WHERE T

SUZANNE STRONG

GREEN ACRE
PUBLISHING

First published in 2019 by Green Acre Publishing, Australia.

This novel is entirely a work of fiction. The names, characters, locations and incidents portrayed in it are the product of the author's imagination. Any resemblance to actual persons, living or dead, is purely coincidental.

Cover Design: May Phan, USA.

ISBN: 13: 978-0-6486732-2-4

For the courageous women who took up arms to fight Daesh and who continue to struggle for freedom, today.

Where the Sun Rises:

'Where the Sun Rises is an ambitious, compassionate and powerful novel. Sensory memories accessed through scents and tastes are used brilliantly to evoke the physical strain, tenderness and revulsion of war for female soldiers in the fight against ISIS. Their story deserves a far wider readership and Strong's achievement lies in her ability to take us into their dangerous world.'

Dr Toby Davidson, Senior Lecturer, English, Macquarie University. From the Kurdish Community

"We Kurdish people are proud of people like you, that are supporting us and are in solidarity with us. It means a lot for us. We know that we have solidarity from all around the world and that makes us stronger. We women are fighting here for all the women not only in Rojava - Syria. Your book is amazing sister. Thank you so much, solidarity greetings from Rojava-Northern-Syria."

YPJ Kurdish Women's Forces Media Centre - October 17, 2018

"Strong has taken care to accurately present the reality of the lives of Kurdish women and the dramatic choices they make as fighters defending their land. The story is remarkable for the authenticity of the detailed portrayal of the geography, the intimate lives of the women fighters and the ferocity of the killing in which they are involved…Strong makes good use of the senses to convey the sounds and smells of battle and death and contrasts it with the delights of singing and dancing, the smell of freshly baked bread and the taste of goat's cheese. The extraordinary amount of research undertaken pays dividends. Recollections of peaceful days and olive groves are neatly woven into the narrative, as are the reassuring pots of tea. Powerful and credible, Where the Sun Rises is an eye-opener to a story we rarely hear."

Dr. Lynne Spender, UTS Lecturer, Sydney.

WHERE THE

SUN RISES

- 1 -

Karin

September 19, 2014,

Kobane, Syria

Karin's long, elegant finger had only one small silver ring on it. She never wore much jewelry; for Karin it only got in her way. Today, she wore jeans and a navy-colored t-shirt, with a dark green jacket and a red scarf around her neck. She leaned over her medical textbook and looked at all the papers strewn across her room.

Closing her thick book, Karin traced the glossy photo outline of the stethoscope dangling over the man's blue shirt, on the cover. A woman in a white coat was standing next to him. Looking at her Karin reflected on the irony that her own desire to save lives might soon be replaced by having to do the opposite. Daesh was moving towards them, and everyone had to decide what they would do. Her parents were against her joining the resistance. For now, she respected their wishes, but no one was going to hurt her family, or take her homeland again, especially not Daesh. She felt as if the blood was thickening in her veins as it coursed through her pounding temple. Moving through the house, Karin walked out onto the verandah, a cold feeling creeping up her spine. Where was her father? As she walked down the steps, the scent of the olive trees surrounded her and she inhaled deeply. It was subtle, but also had a sharp effect on the senses. Walking across the field, she felt the balmy afternoon on her arms, and heard the chimes of birds calling, like a cascading waterfall, through the olive groves on their land. The spindly branches of the trees darkened against the landscape as the sun prepared to set over Kobane. Karin saw that the surrounding hills were now touched with the slightest color of peach, pink, and pale blue.

A longing came over her, as she remembered playing with her brother Ahman in these groves, laughing, climbing, and falling off the brittle limbs. Karin's family had a twelve-acre farm near the hills of Western Kobane. Now, Karin felt a dark shadow hanging over her home, and over the future of this place. Her place, their place; it could be taken from them again. Karin felt her jaw tighten as she walked further. This was her family's land; her grandfather had passed it down to them. As she walked, the woody, strong scent of the bark filled her senses, and she picked one of the small khaki leaves from the twig of a dark branch. Crushing it and putting it to her nose, Karin drank in its smell. Wandering further along the path, she found her father Aster, smoking his shisha pipe and sitting on the wooden bench that looked out into the trees. She approached him quietly, as it was unusual to see him out here on his own.

"Babo." She touched him from behind. "Are you okay?"

"Yes, Kar. I'm fine." He motioned to he thinking about everything, and wondering how long we have *them* on our doorstep."

"Me too," Karin said, sitting. "I was watching the news, and they are only a few kilometers from here. Have you changed your mind about me joining the fight?"

"No. Kar. Mani will, but not you. It would kill your mother."

"You know I've always wanted to fight for our people. I know I could do it…"

"Stop. That's enough. I don't want to talk about it anymore. You'll be a doctor one day, and Mani is young and strong. It's not right for you to go…" He said, looking directly into her eyes.

"Why? Cause I'm female? We've had women in the army for years. You're always telling me I can do anything, but you only mean certain things…"

"It's because *I* don't want you to go," he said quietly. "I couldn't bear it." He looked away and blew a long stream of grey smoke into the cool air.

Karin touched his arm. "You may have to–one day."

He did not speak anymore, and neither did Karin. He gave her a puff on his shisha, saying, "Don't tell your mother," and winking. It was forbidden for women to smoke. *Another ridiculous restriction placed on us, not men.* They both looked into the olive trees lined up in perfect formation. Karin

...bered the times she climbed the spindly branches to the top, ...a even when she was about to fall, Aster would allow her to keep climbing. He wasn't fearful. She hated what Daesh was doing to her people. Why couldn't she fight? Karin heard her mother calling them for dinner, from the house. They stood up and crept back.

"Where were you, sis?" Ahman said, ruffling her hair.

"Outside..." she said, putting her arm around him in a sisterly embrace.

"Well, you took your time. We were waiting to eat." He smiled mischievously.

She plonked herself down onto the cushion on the floor. Her mother had made some dolma, chicken, rice, salad, and a pot of tea that was on the mat. She looked at her mother, and then they all bowed.

"Bismillah," Aster said, "In the name of Allah."

Karin looked up and began to serve Mani first, offering him some salad and goat's cheese. Passing him the bread, she put some on her own plate, as well as chunks of white cheese. She gathered some cucumber together with a section of the salty, cheese, and felt it crumble and mingle in her mouth. Between bites she poured the tea into small glass cups, for Mani, her parents, and herself.

"Are you still studying, Kar?" her mother, Maia asked.

"Hm, yes, Mama. I've been a bit distracted, though, by everything. I've put everything on hold after I had to cancel my exam in Damascus last week."

"Very true, love. We don't want you traveling if it's dangerous, and Daesh is definitely on the move."

"It is, and we will meet them wherever they are," Ahman said, as he put some chicken into his mouth.

"Yes, we will, *Xwa* willing," Aster said, looking at Karin.

Karin remained silent. Inside, she was infuriated that her parents would not allow her to fight. Since she was a young child, she'd followed the struggles of her people fighting for their Kurdish lands. Karin saw herself when she was little, sitting next to Aster, listening to his deep, rough voice explain about her Kurdish heritage. He talked about how their people fought for their land after the First World War, when their ancient culture and lands were absorbed into other countries' borders.

"You will be able to study again, sis. Once we defeat them. *Xwa* willing, it will be quick," Mani said.

"Who knows? Yes, *Xwa* willing, it will be quick, and you'll be safe, Mani." She touched his forearm and looked into his eyes with a serious, but tender, gaze.

"Yes, thanks, sis," he said.

After packing up the dishes, washing the plates, and putting them on the sink to dry, Karin and Ahman went outside into the crisp night air. Sitting at the top of their farm on a hill, Ahman took out his tobacco, and offered Karin a cigarette. She accepted. She didn't always smoke, but she had done it a lot more with Ahman lately, since everything in Kobane had become extremely serious. Karin licked the paper and sealed the cylindrical white tube of tobacco. She lit it up, and felt a slight head-spin as she exhaled out into the night. They both sat silently looking out at the horizon. Lately, the sound of war had echoed in the distance, and it seemed to be advancing towards them, moving ever closer. Right now, the day was fading into beautiful colors, soft and gentle and the call of the white-and fawn-speckled Isabelline Wheatear bird could be heard echoing across the valley. Neither of them wanted to speak; they knew what the other was thinking. Would Mani be okay, when he joined the resistance? Would Karin be able to stand not joining?

"I'm not afraid, Kar," he said, abruptly breaking the silence.

"I know you're not, Mani. You've always been brave."

Karin saw her brother as a little chubby toddler, playing with his wooden car, his black hair like a round bowl on top of his head. Then as he got older, she remembered him with his slingshot in the grove, how accurate he became with it, precise and deadly.

"Thanks," Ahman said, looking straight ahead. His jaw clenched, then flexed and released. Karin recognized this, she had seen it before when Mani faced Rivin Hossein that afternoon in the dusty, alleyway near the school. Karin was across the road, but she saw Mani's jaw set as Rivin towered over him. Then they began to fight. Mani was throwing punches, and Rivin was hitting him in the face and stomach. Then they both began to kick at each other. Karin had run across the road and pushed their small bodies

14

apart. She had threatened Rivin that he would have to deal with her if he ever picked on Mani again. Mani was annoyed at first, but later, Karin could tell he was pleased.

"It's okay though, if you're scared," she said now. "I would be. Who wouldn't?" Ahman did not answer. He faced ahead and exhaled circles into the air. Karin didn't expect him to say much—he didn't need to. They sat together and smoked, Karin reveling in this quiet moment with her brother. They hadn't had much time together, the two of them alone, since she'd started university five years ago.

**

"Have you got everything we need, Mani?"

"Think so," Mani answered Karin.

Walking out of the store at the markets, Karin bumped into Sozan. Her friend looked at her intensely, and asked how she was. They had been friends since they were fifteen. Growing up together, Karin had seen Sozan in the tumultuous years of teenage life. She had rebelled against her violent, abusive father, and left home at sixteen to live with her Aunty and Uncle. Karin looked into Sozan's face, her light green eyes startling beneath dyed blonde hair, and saw one of the strongest women she knew.

"If Daesh comes, Karin, I'm joining the fight," Sozan said, following Mani and Karin outside of the shop.

"Me too," Mani said.

Karin looked at them both, envious that they could so confidently state this, but also worried for them.

"Are you sure, Soz?

"Yes, Kar. You know me. I have never shied away from a fight." Sozan laughed, but Karin could tell she wasn't entirely comfortable. Who could be? Karin didn't know what to say.

"My parents want to stay in Kobane. I want to join too, but they won't let me."

"Oh, well, it's right that you do what they want."

"Maybe. It's hard, though. Anyway, will I see you before you go?" Karin asked.

"No, probably not. We have to move fast. I guess this is goodbye for now—and hopefully, see you soon." Sozan embraced Karin and kissed her three times. Karin felt this might be the last time she would see Sozan.

"Be careful, love," Karin said.

"You too, Kar."

"Be safe, may *Xwa* be with you."

"And with you, also. Talk to you soon. Bye, Mani."

"Bye, Sozan. See you on the frontline."

"Yes, you will." Sozan saluted them both before walking off. Karin felt Sozan was being too light-hearted about this. She turned and started walking towards home with Mani. It wasn't surprising that Sozan was joining the resistance. She had always been the angriest, most independent woman Karin knew.

Mani and Karin began to walk back home through the streets. They had purchased rice, tea, and sugar. Mani whistled, as he often did, and began to tell Karin about Lasia, the girl he liked. Karin smiled to herself. There was a big gap in age between them; he was twenty, and Karin was twenty-six, and their conversations were gradually becoming more adult. When they reached the hill just before their house and farm, they heard a sound that made them stop. It was shellfire and bombing. In the distance, not that far away, massive explosions of white soil and concrete formed clouds on the horizon, flying high into the sky. Inside, Karin simultaneously felt fear and outrage, sick at heart that Daesh would come and seek to conquer them, as so many other peoples had done before. Karin pulled Ahman close to herself.

"That must be Ghasaniyeh. It's very close now," Ahman said.

Karin nodded. "We should get home to talk to Mama and Dad."

When they got home, their parents were watching the news on television. The black flag flapped in the wind; the footage was from the neighboring town to Kobane.

"It appears Daesh is moving and covering more ground, and has now entered the town of Ghasaniyeh. There is resistance from the Kurdish people, but it appears Daesh has conquered this town," a dark-haired, female journalist, with furrowed brows, said. The map of Syria in the graphics behind her showed Karin's town of Kobane.

"Officials are worried that Daesh may seek to overtake Kobane. This would be a terrible thing in the war against Daesh. If

Daesh takes control of Kobane, the group will have 60 miles stretching from the Euphrates River to the border with Turkey. It is a strategic town, and is near many oil reserves, and it would be disastrous if Daesh captures this land. This would allow them to gain a major position of strength…" The woman's voice trailed off, and Karin's thoughts turned to Roza, her best friend since they were five years old. She decided she would ring Roza the next day to see how she was going. Roza must have been distraught, especially for her son, Yez. Karin's mind was like a goat roaming over the side of a mountain, seeking footholds in precariously small spaces. They were close; it was happening. What were they going to do? She couldn't voice out loud about what she wanted to do. At least, not now.

- 2 -

Roza

September 19, 2014,

Kobane, Syria

"Get dressed, sweetheart, it's time for school," said Roza. She touched Yezdanser's straight black hair. "Okay, just finishing this…" Yezdanser held up his half-made paper airplane. He folded his last section with a look of concentration and his tongue sticking out of his mouth slightly. Roza loved this expression of his. He raised the plane above his head and released it into the air. It ascended for a few moments and then plummeted into a nosedive onto the multi-colored, intricately patterned rug. He laughed. Yez shoveled his last spoonful of egg into his mouth, spilling it onto his plate, and then took a small sip of lukewarm, sweet tea.

"You can do that later." She gathered some fruit together in a paper bag for him.

Roza's husband, Sercan, walked into their small kitchen behind her. He embraced her from behind and kissed her on the cheek. "I have to go. I'll be home around 4:30pm," he said. Sercan worked in Jusef's hardware shop in the main street.

"Have a good day," Roza said, trying to sound normal for Yez's sake. She did not want to believe everything she loved could be destroyed. It was all she had ever wanted. Sercan hugged Yez. "Have a good day, sonny boy." She helped Yez up from the kitchen table; he was always hard to get moving in the morning. After getting him into his jeans, t-shirt, and jacket, and giving him his lunch, she drove him through Kobane to the small white building of the Yarmouk School.

Roza felt proud that her son could learn Kurdish at school, this luxury was only possible since they had won this region back from the Regime in 2012, as part of Rojava. It had been a long fight for her people, but walking Yez into the school, she knew it was worth it. For the past two years in Kobane, her people had experienced the freedom to express their culture, which had been denied them for the previous sixty years.

There was always a specter over them, however, and Roza wasn't naïve. She preferred to not think about Daesh and what it could mean for her family. She had just started a job teaching English and History, in the Eastern Kobane High School. The Kurdish woman at the reception greeted Roza, and they kissed twice on each cheek.

"Morning. Great to see you both," Mrs. Jenin said, "The class is small today as some people are worried about what's happening, and they've started to leave Kobane."

"Really? Is it that bad already?" Roza asked, pulling Yez closer to herself.

"Well, they're getting closer. Very close." Mrs Jenin moved a paper on the table between them, she glanced quickly at Yez.

"Is Yez safe here? Should I take him home?"

"It's up to you. We'll keep him safe, though."

"I think maybe I'll take him with me. We'll see, maybe he can come tomorrow."

"Okay. I understand." Mrs Jenin managed a tentative smile. Lines formed on her forehead as Roza could tell she was concerned but also relieved Roza was not leaving him.

"I'm sorry. I don't like Yez to miss school."

"I know you don't. But there's nothing we can do at the moment, unfortunately, is there?"

"No, that's true. I'll ring in the morning to see what's happening."

"Be safe, Roza. Bye, Yez." Mrs Jenin waved at him as they left. He waved back. They left and Roza drove to her parents' house, as Yez asked her why he wasn't going to school. She said the holidays were coming and some of the teachers were away. Roza knew this was not convincing Yez, but what could she say? *There are people coming to Kobane who want us dead.* Her school had been temporarily closed. On the way to her parents' home, Roza called Karin, her closest friend, who said she shouldn't worry too much, but that she made the right decision taking Yez home. Roza knocked on her parent's door. This had been Roza's home her whole life, and she didn't want to leave it. She grew up here from the age of five. She couldn't believe that if Daesh came too close, they might have to leave all of this behind, never to return. It was a humble building, with white-washed rough concrete walls and exterior. Inside the house, there were photographs of their family life, her parents, her cousins, marriages, and the birth of Yez. In the lounge room, there was a large wooden cabinet that held albums of photographs of Yez growing up, taken by her parents. On top of it were vases and pottery, and her favorite china cup, the one her grandma gave her when she was four years old. It had a chip in its base, and a blue and yellow flower painted delicately on the side. How could they leave all of this? All of their lives were here. They would never be able to take everything with them. She hoped it didn't come to that.

"This is a surprise. Are you and Yez okay?" Roza's mother, Naze, asked when she opened the door.

"Yes, kind of. Yez can't go to school–he has to stay home, there's hardly anyone there."

"No problems. Come in. You can have your nanna's flatbread and honey, Yez."

Naze took Yez's hand and walked him into the kitchen. Roza couldn't shake a feeling of dread, almost as if she had been winded, like when someone kicks a chair out from under you. She rang Sercan on his mobile.

"Hello, sweet. I had to take Yez out of school."

"Really?" Sercan asked, "Because of Daesh?"

"Yes. We need to talk when you get home about what we're going to do."

"We will. I'll try to get home early."

"Please do. I don't feel great, Ser. I love you."

"I love you," he said. "I'll be home as soon as possible." Roza hung up. She felt slightly sick for the rest of the day, and stayed with her mother. Roza allowed Yez to have their neighbor Assan over for two hours to play, with their soldier figurines and soccer ball. They liked to play war games, which now made Roza feel uncomfortable, with how close it was to their reality. Roza rang Karin again; she was always reassuring when things weren't going very well.

"*Silav,* how are you, Kar with all of this?"

"*Silav,* I'm okay, Rozi. How are things going over there?"

"I'm worried. Yez is with me. Are you going to leave?"

"I don't think our family are. We can't leave Kobane. Daesh is advancing quicker than anyone expected. But we will fight them. We won't surrender Kobane, not after everything we've been through. Mani and I saw the explosions today on our way home. It was so close, Roz."

"Yes. I didn't want to believe it was happening. I hoped we would have received more help from the Regime or other countries. But, nothing."

"Yes, no one to help us, we're used to this. My family are staying, and Mani is going to the frontline to fight them." There was silence on the phone.

"I wish I could join Mani, but I can't. I don't want to distress them," Karin continued.

"I'm glad you're not going to the frontline. I think my parents want to stay as well; they don't think there is any other option. Dad thinks he's too old to cross the border. He said he would rather stay in Kobane and die here if he has to. We don't know what to expect over the border either. We have to defend Kobane. I'm afraid Ser will join the fight as well. We haven't talked yet."

"Well, wait and see what he says. Did you talk to Sozan? I saw her the other day. She is joining the people who are fighting as well."

"Really? That's not surprising for Soz. It's not like we could talk her out of anything ever." Roza laughed, then stopped herself. It didn't feel right to laugh about what was happening to them all.

"Yes, that's definitely true. I didn't even try."

"I'll ring her phone; do you think she will still have it?"

"Yes, I'm sure she would."

"Good. I want to know she's okay."

"Good idea. How are your parents?"

"They're okay, considering. Dad is distant and quiet as usual. He's not saying much, and Ma wants to stay, but she is worried as well."

"My parents are afraid, as well."

"Okay, I'm so glad you'll be with me here in Kobane. I wouldn't want to do this without you. Do you think we are doing the right thing?" Roza asked.

"I feel the same. I'm glad you will be here. You know how I feel. I want to fight. I feel better staying closer to Mani and in Kobane. I don't want to flee."

"I agree, I feel better being close to Ser if he chooses to fight. Someone has to stand up to Daesh and defend our home. I just pray Ser will be kept safe."

"Me too. And for Mani, as well. Who knows? Maybe Daesh won't make it into the town. Maybe we will successfully fight them off."

"Yes, you never know."

"Well, love, I'll call you later to see how you're going. Love you. Take care."

"Love you too. Be careful." Roza hung up. She dialed Sozan's number praying she would pick up. It kept ringing and ringing, Roza began to feel sick. She was about to hang up when she heard Sozan's voice, cavalier and casual.

"Rozi!" she said in an excited and warm tone.

"Soz, how are you?"

"I'm good. How are you, and little Yez?"

"Yez is okay. He doesn't understand what is happening."

"Well, that's probably a good thing. Poor little darling. Can you give him a kiss for me?"

"Of course." Roza felt sad listening to Sozan's voice. No one knew what would happen.

"Did you know I'm joining the resistance? Did Karin tell you?"

"Yes, Karin told me."

"Yeah, I saw her and Mani the other day."

"Are you sure you should, Soz?"

"I'm more sure about this than anything I've ever done."

"Okay. I'm worried for you, though."

"I know. My Aunt and Uncle were concerned too. I had to leave them without their blessing. But they know once I get something in my mind, they can't tell me what to do. I'm my own person."

"Yes, you are, Soz."

"My Mum called my Aunt. She was worried as well, but you know I don't have much contact with them. They will have to accept it. It's what I feel I am meant to do. I'm so sure, Roz."

"Okay, I understand. I think my parents feel they can't and don't want to leave Kobane. I would like them to leave, but I think their minds are made up. I haven't talked to Ser, but we will stay here with them."

"Oh, really? But you should go. It will be safer for all of you over the border."

"I know, but sometimes my father gets very stubborn. You never know. Maybe Daesh won't make it right into our town." Roza knew her voice didn't sound convincing.

"Yes, true. None of us know what will happen, do we? I'll do everything I can to keep them out of Kobane. I found out the other day that my mother said they haven't heard from Ashti. She was coming back from Damascus, and they don't know where she is."

"Oh, no! That's terrible."

"They will find her. I'm sure she's with friends and just can't get in contact. Maybe she doesn't have access to a phone."

"I pray that's the case, Soz."

"Me too. I'll pray for them all when I think of them and for our deliverance from Daesh. God will help us; I know it."

"I believe, but I'm scared."

"I know. It's terrifying. I would rather go and fight than do nothing, though. I don't want others to continue to die at the hands of these men, not anymore."

"Hopefully, you'll be able to get help from the YPG."

"Yes, we're communicating. Right now, it seems the civilians are on their own, there's no one to help us. I'll need some instruction on how to use the weaponry, but I will get it."

"Yes, you will, Soz. I know you will. Ser and Mani are also going to be on the Eastern side of Kobane. I have to go, Soz. But I want you to know I'm thinking of you and praying for your safety and the deliverance of us all."

"*Zor spas*, Rozi, me too. Hopefully, I'll see you soon. May God be with you."

"Thank you, and you too." Roza hung up. She felt a sinking feeling in her stomach as she walked outside and watched Yez and Assan play soccer in their small yard. The boys had constructed imaginary goals out of their shoes and ran in bare feet. Naze came outside, bringing them tea in a small, dark green teapot and two small cups.

They sat in silence, watching the boys. Yez scored a goal and ran to Roza, yelling, "Yes!" and running around in circles. He ran into her arms for a congratulatory hug. She embraced his small frame and rested her head on his little shoulders. Then, Yez ran off, joining the game with Assan again. Roza knew this could be the last time their lives would be as normal as this.

***

Later that afternoon, Sercan came to Roza's parents' house. When he came in, the whole family was watching the news. Roza and her parents sat on cushions on the floor. When he arrived, Roza got up and kissed him, then signaled for him to look at the television.

"Daesh has now entered the outskirts of the Kobane Kanton…" Footage of tanks rolling forward and shelling, of black flags flailing in the wind, men running down streets and laneways with grenade launchers and machine guns. Roza watched in shock as the reality of their situation played like a horror film on the television screen. Only this wasn't fiction, Roza could no longer pretend it wasn't happening.

Naze gasped as they showed people being lined up on the edge of the Euphrates and shot in the back of the head, their bodies crumpling and falling like limp, rag dolls into the river. Footage of just before they beheaded men and women kneeling with black bags over their heads, with fast-paced menacing music playing in the background. The broadcast cut off before the act of violence, but Roza was still horrified. These were people, and Daesh was shooting them and discarding them like trash. A blinding headache attacked Roza's forehead, sending sharp pain behind her eyes and above her nose.

"Ser, please take Yez out of here. He can't see this."

Roza's father, Bazan, got up and walked out of the house as well to have a smoke. Sercan and Yez went into the yard.

"What are we going to do, Ma? Things are getting very dark here."

"Yes, Roz, but I don't want to go yet. You never know, things may not get as bad as we think. Besides, what would Ocalan say? He would say to fight for our homeland."

"Yes, I know you're right." Roza's mother had raised her reading Abdullah Ocalan's writings about the autonomy of her people and a socialist, democratic Kurdish state.

"Good."

Roza could not take her eyes off the news as it showed the hills that surrounded them on the south-east of Kobane. She realized it would only be a matter of days before they would be on their doorstep. Roza suddenly felt heat all over her body and sick in the stomach. She got up and went to find Sercan and Yez.

- 3 -

Karin

September 21 - October 5, 2014

"Babo, what are we going to do? Many are leaving over the border." Karin looked out their window onto the street where hundreds of her neighbors were walking, carrying large bags and sacks of belongings, their children walking beside them or carried on their backs. Chaos had gripped Kobane in the last two days. Daesh had moved in closer from all directions, and was attacking the villages surrounding their town.

"I know, Kar. But I don't want to. I want to stay here, near Mani. This is our place. I can't leave it. You know everything we have fought for all these years, and now, finally, Kobane is a Kurdish territory. You, of all people, would know how I feel about this." For the first time, Karin heard a quiver in his voice.

"I know, Papa," she said, "but I don't want anything to happen to you. You've heard what they did to that man in Mamit who stayed. He was 74; they beheaded him in front of his wife and three children. Then they put it on the internet. She's gone and his three children as well. They're so close; what if they enter Kobane?"

"I know, but maybe they won't. I think we should stay. Some civilians are staying. What other option do we have? Go over to Turkey as a refugee? No, I don't want to be a refugee, homeless again. I have a rifle; I will use it to defend my family."

It was like Aster had been cemented into his position in the corner of the room. His apple tobacco scent filled the lounge room. Maia sat silently on her cushion, sipping a small cup of tea.

"Mama." Karin turned to Maia.

"Yes, dear."

"Do you agree with him?"

"I want to stay near my son. Where is Ahman?" Maia asked.

"He's with the people who are going to fight," Karin answered.

"Is he?" she said. Karin continued to look outside and nodded. So, her family didn't want to leave. It didn't seem as if they knew how serious this was, but she could understand them not wanting to as well. She didn't want to either. What she did want, more than anything, was to take up arms. She had wanted to do this since she was a young girl when Aster would talk about the struggles her people had and how they had to defend themselves.

Later that day, Ahman came home and started getting his things together. He said he was moving to the outskirts of the city where the civilian Kurdish men and women were positioning themselves in buildings, waiting to fight off Daesh as they approached.

"Do you have to join up, Mani? What would I do if something bad happened?" Maia said, tracing his cheek with her hand.

"I have to, Mama, we have no choice. Who will defend Kobane, otherwise?" She grabbed hold of him and hugged him as tight as Karin had ever seen, sobbing quietly into his shoulder. Karin walked over.

"May *Xwa* be with you, Mani. I will pray for you every day. You're strong and brave." Karin's eyes watered. "I'll be here, right here. We're not leaving. I'm ready to join right alongside you, brother. For the moment, I'll take care of our parents."

"You're staying in Kobane? Is that a good idea?" Mani's face darkened like a brewing thunderstorm overhead. "Maybe you should leave over the border like everyone else. It's open at the moment, but we don't know how long it will be."

Maia touched his shoulder and spoke quietly. "Our place is here. We'll be here, near you. Kobane is our place. Be strong, son. We're all with you in spirit. So proud of you."

"Ma." Mani hugged her again, more concern in his voice now, but resigned to the fact that they wouldn't change their minds. "Look after Ma and Papa, they need you," he said, turning to Karin.

"We'll see you soon. Hopefully, this will be over quickly. We'll be here, waiting for you and we may be able to see you sometime." He smiled and nodded, though both of them didn't look convinced. Karin looked into his eyes, kissed him four times, and held him tightly. His shoulders seemed smaller and bonier than before, vulnerable somehow. She wanted him to be large and bulky, and felt a terrible dread of wanting to protect him but knowing she couldn't. It was unbearable. Mani gathered his things and left the house. Karin watched his small body as he went out onto the street and jumped onto the back of the utility vehicle that would take him away. The men greeted him, and he turned back towards Karin, smiling his boyish, mischievous smirk under his patchy new beard. For a moment, Karin saw him as a ten-year-old boy. He formed the victory sign with two fingers as they drove off down the dusty white street. Despite this, Karin noticed a seriousness in his eyes she had never seen before and felt she might never see again.

It was getting dark. Karin had watched the news the day before. Daesh had filmed themselves running down the streets coming from the south-east and west of Kobane, machine guns slung over their shoulders, and now and then they would stop and launch a grenade into a building. They moved into their area with tanks and heavy artillery. In the neighboring towns, women and young girls were being stolen and reports of beheadings reaching Kobane.

Nearly 200,000 people were crossing over the border into Turkey, according to the news. Karin felt proud they were part of the thousand people who had stayed within Kobane. From their house, they watched the procession of people leaving on the streets. In the following two weeks, Karin would go out with her mother, wearing a headscarf even though it wasn't normal for her. They had to get food from neighbors and check how everyone was going. It also allowed them to find out what was happening on the frontline. Those who stayed in Kobane banded together sharing their food and visiting abandoned shops for bread, blankets, sugar, supplies of any type. Fruit, vegetables, and even meat, were commonly shared by all of them. There was a baker who had stayed in Kobane as well to support those who were resisting. Often Karin, Roza, and Yez would find themselves at his bakery, listening to the people sharing information from the frontline.

As time went by, Karin knew they would have to seek food from further afield if the battle continued. They knew they could smuggle food over the border as they had people over there. Roza, Karin, and Yez would walk down the deserted streets of Kobane. Karin would carry Yez, and he would wrap his tiny arms firmly around her neck as they walked around their side of Kobane. One morning Karin saw a small pink, stuffed elephant with a charred face, lying in the dirt and it seemed like a symbol of the decimation of this war. Domestic life, singed and destroyed. She glanced over at Roza to see if she had noticed. Today, Karin thought, she looked particularly frail. She remembered Roza's unassuming nature as a teenager, how she would often lower her light brown eyes, avoiding the gaze of strangers, behind a mass of black, wavy hair. Roza glanced back and smiled, and Karin saw the small scar, half an inch long, above her eye. It reminded her of that night when they were seventeen and Roza turned up on her doorstep. It was raining, and when she had opened the front door, Roza's wet, disheveled figure stood there forlorn and crying. Blood was pouring out of a gash above her eye, as she held a small cloth to her face.

Karin had gasped when she saw Roza. Her flesh was swollen, with red and deep grey coloring her cheek. Her words had been like Roza was, small, and quiet. "Help me, Kar." Karin remembered pulling her inside; she knew it would have been her uncle. He often did this when he was drunk, and her parents were out of town. Patting Roza's face with disinfectant, Karin had placed a cotton ball on her eye to stop the bleeding. Placing an ice block onto her face, she sought to numb the skin. Roza was crying, but Karin remained focused, swallowing large lumps of emotion in the back of her throat. Karin's Uncle Asgher was a doctor, and he had taught her how to do this in his surgery. It was different when it was your closest friend, though.

Despite this, Karin had set about preparing her mother's needle and thread. Placing the needle over the top of Roza's skin, she hesitated, then forced herself to make the incision, a sharp, small hole into her friend's pale, thin skin. As she pulled the thread through softly, Roza flinched and cried out, and then stopped herself. Karin continued, carefully and delicately closing the gap in her skin. Tears rolled down Roza's cheeks. When she had finished, Karin tied it off. The next day they would go to a doctor, but for now, Karin pulled her close for a hug and placed a blanket around her shoulders. Her mother poured them some hot tea. They didn't speak much, just sat together.

***

A week later, Karin was picking up some oranges from the neighbor; she smelt the fresh, citrus bite of its skin as she put it into her bag. Asgher came up to her. She wondered why he looked upset. Did we need more rice? Were her parents okay? He whispered something in her ear, and the orange fell from her hand,

36

bouncing heavily into the dirt of the front yard. A sharp sensation crossed her temple as she took in his words.

"Behea...dead... no! That's not..." She became breathless and felt pain shooting from the bottom of her neck all through her head. "No!" she said again, as if someone would answer her. Then she fell completely silent. Inside, she was screaming. Her blood was congealing in her organs, and she felt she would vomit. Running back through the streets, she eventually reached the rock-laden path that led to their farm. The back of her throat ached from her breathlessness. She moved across the rocks in a fury and then slowed herself down, deciding it was better to approach slowly. Karin felt frantic about her parents. Her uncle had told her they captured Mani in close fighting with Daesh. Karin felt sick that she hadn't been there for him. *My little brother...* Karin whispered to herself as if the reality could not be true. On a hill on the eastern side of Kobane, Daesh beheaded Mani and filmed the horror as well.

Once Karin got to the house, she walked into the lounge room, but her mother was not there. Karin crept into the bedroom. Maia was sitting silently, her face lifeless as darkness permeated the room. Karin's father sat on a cushion in the corner; she embraced him. His face looked forlorn and lost, bewildered, as if the world had suddenly become the blackest tunnel and he couldn't see through its depths. No one spoke. What could they say? Karin couldn't say anything; she wanted to scream, not talk. Her mother got up from the cushion and walked to a mattress on the floor. Karin followed her. She watched Maia kneel slowly and fall face down as if dead. Then her mother cried a high-pitched sound that Karin had never heard. Her cries were deep and breathless. Karin began to weep, breathless sobs, hugging her mother. She nudged her mother to turn over, and she did. Her mother's face was broken; her eyes dead from the black center out. She turned and lay on her side and sobbed quietly. Karin embraced her mother and lay there for a while, seeing Mani's beautiful face. He couldn't be gone.

She wept for her brother; for the boy who wanted to be a builder when he was older, who was always drawing and entertaining them. His imitations of the accents of merchants and his stupid jokes played over in her mind. His face appeared before her, his eyes with their humorous mischievousness, warm above his crooked smile. Karin and Ahman had been called twins when they were young, even though there was the six-year age gap. They were inseparable. She would fight for Ahman, of course, she would. There was nothing left to do. She no longer cared about her life; she would gladly give it for him. No longer would she sit by and watch Kobane be violated in this way. They had taken Mani, but they would not take everything. She would fight now, for Aster, Maia and Mani's honor. *They will bloody well pay for this*.

She got up from the bed and went to Mani's chest of drawers, found a pair of his khaki military pants, and put them on. He was tall, and the pants were baggy, but she zipped them up and walked outside. Grabbing an aluminum can sitting on a nearby rock, Karin threw it as hard as she could against the stone wall as rage filled every part of her. It clattered and threw dirt everywhere. She pushed over a wooden seat. Rage filled every part of her.

"Stop, Karin," Uncle Asgher said behind her. "Remember what the Quran says about mourning."

"I don't care," she whispered, disdain in her voice.

He walked closer, touched her but she turned away. She crouched down close to the earth and wept. He pulled up the seat and ushered her to sit down, but she refused and signaled to his cigarettes on his lap. He hesitated, then handed the packet to her as she moved towards him. She sat down in the dirt and lit up. Karin remembered sneaking off with Roza one morning to try smoking, her head spinning behind the corrugated iron shed as they coughed and giggled together. Now, her head spun again. It felt both rebellious and liberating, and now, strangely, it briefly relieved her rage. After a little while, Karin entered the house again to speak to Aster. They went and sat outside on the veranda.

"You know what I'm going to say, don't you?"

Aster nodded; he looked straight ahead.

"I can no longer stay. I know Mama doesn't want me to go, but I'm a woman now. You can't stop me, Dad." Aster looked into her face, his lips quivered and tears were forming in his eyes. Karin's eyes flooded as well. It made her ache inside to see his light, hazel eyes bloodshot and filled with tears. His face was downcast.

He took her hand firmly in his. "I know, little one. You want to go. I could never stop you doing anything when you were set on it. Remember, you and Mani had been determined to build that boat out of wood and to carve it yourself? I said you wouldn't be able to do it properly."

"I remember," she replied.

"Then, after three days of hard work and many mistakes, you did it. You were determined, and you did it, Kar." He shook his head as if he still didn't believe it. His voice was shaky.

"And now, Mani is gone…how can we lose you too?" He began to weep, quietly. Karin's throat ached. She stood up slowly and touched his shoulder.

"I know. But I can't stay any longer, doing nothing. I can't do this anymore." Karin wiped away the tears that were lining her cheeks, feeling irritated with them. "I will leave in a week. It's not fair to leave you now."

"Thank you, Kar," Aster said, taking her hand to his face and kissing it. "We'll have to tell your Ma."

"Can you tell her tomorrow or the next day? I can't." Karin looked down. She did not want Aster to see the pain in her eyes and couldn't bear to face her mother's anguish.

"Yes."

"You need to move with the other people into the safe part of Kobane or go over the border. I don't want anything to happen to you."

"We can talk about that later. I don't care about my life now. Mani is gone." Aster began to weep. Karin embraced him, and they cried together, their anguish and anger mingling. She knew she was breaking their hearts, but she prayed *Xwa* would protect her and allow her to see them again. Mani had not been so fortunate; she hoped *Xwa* was with him in those last moments and had taken him to paradise, though she was no longer sure of what she believed. Inside there was a fire. It had been like a small smoldering flicker at first, but now, Karin felt it growing and becoming a roaring, wild, uncontrollable force. She imagined the men who would dare to come in and murder her brother cold-heartedly. Were they even human? No one would stop her from joining now. Maybe if she had been there, she could have protected him. Now if she died, she at least knew she was fighting for his honor and their family.

***

A few days later Karin contacted the Yekîneyên Parastina Jin (YPJ)—the female volunteer unit of Syrian Kurdish militia—and told them she wanted to enlist. She went to see Roza and told her she was leaving. The following day, she said goodbye to Aster and Maia, and made sure they had plans to move to a safer place. Karin had explained to Roza she was joining the fight. Her friend had not been surprised since Karin had talked about nothing else in the past few weeks. Roza always understood; she would miss her. Karin assured Roz she was fighting for her and their families. Maia had accepted her daughter's decision, but not without tears and yelling.

Karin embraced her mother's shaking body. "Love you, Mama, *so* much."

"May *Xwa* protect you, precious one, and bring you back to me. I love you too.*"*

Karin kissed her mother on her cheeks and held her tightly. She embraced her father and breathed in his earthy tobacco smell. Karin held him tight.

"I have something for you, Kar. It's Mani's leather band bracelet. He gave you one, and he had one for himself, remember? I think you should wear it, and you will always be connected," Aster said.

Karin looked at it and sought to hold back the emotion. "That's a lovely idea, Dad. I'll always wear it. I have mine, but I would rather wear his." She put it onto her wrist and touched its softness.

"I'll see you soon, when Kobane is free. May Mani rest in peace. Tell Roza I'll contact her as soon as I can."

"Okay." Maia blew a kiss, but tried not to show any emotion. Aster looked at the ground as Karin jumped onto the car that would take her to the YPJ training camp on the other side of Kobane. There she would begin a grueling training regime to prepare her for the brutal combat she would face. Nothing could adequately prepare her for it, though. Every day she prayed for her parents, even though she wondered if there was any point, as God seemed silent to her. She dreaded the thought of how her parents would cope if she was killed. Mani's death would not be for nothing; she would make damn sure of it.

- 4 -

Roza

Kobane

September 21 -October 9, 2014

"I can't let you fight, Ser. What about Yez and me?"

"I have to. No one else is going to help us. What do you expect me to do? If I don't fight, I'll feel like I let you both down."

"You wouldn't have. You don't have to prove anything to me."

"I know."

Sercan embraced Roza. She buried her head into his shoulder, and smelt the sweet sweat scent of his skin, mixed with oil and diesel from the hardware shop. It was strange to Roza that she had come to love this smell. Her father was a mechanic, so it was familiar. He had taught her how to change the oil in the car, alongside the shock absorbers, and anything else she cared to know. Roza remembered how curious she was as a kid. She had become an English teacher, very different to her father's side of the family. She was like her mother, who always read voraciously, and who had introduced her to Abdullah Ocalan when she was ten years old.

Roza looked into Ser's large dark eyes. He always had this look, when he regarded her, that communicated a deep tenderness. She could hardly bear to look at him now. What if she lost him? They had been together since she was eighteen. Tall and broad-shouldered, Sercan was strong and formidable in his appearance. It was his gentleness, however, that had instantly drawn Roza to him. Her childhood of domestic violence from her uncle, who lived with them, had made her like a flighty, delicate swallow, one who barely touched the ground, always ready to fly free. Sercan though, was different from most men she met. Now, she just wanted to stay in his arms, always. Sercan produced a purple and black checked scarf from behind his back.

"I bought this for you on my way home. I know you've been looking at it for a while, but you're always so careful with our money."

"Oh, you didn't need to, Ser. But thanks, it's lovely." She took it and touched her face with it. Roza never wore a headscarf but loved wearing scarves. She began to fasten it around her neck, and Sercan stood behind her and tied it gently up.

"You can think of me when you wear it. Until I see you again."

"I will." Roza turned and kissed him tenderly on the mouth, tears fell onto her lips. "I can't bear this."

"I know, sweetheart. I'll have to leave soon. They're very close, Roz. I pray that you will be kept safe. I couldn't stand if anything happened to either of you."

Yez came into the room. He looked at them.

"Mama," he said as a question more than a noun.

"Yes, sweetheart. Everything is okay. Papa is going to join the fight to protect us."

"Okay, does he have to?" Yez asked, beginning to get emotional. Sercan leaned down with tears in his eyes and picked up his son.

"I have to fight, Yez. But I'll see you soon. I'll only be on the other side of Kobane. You will be here with Mama. Can you take care of her for me?"

"Yes, Papa." Yez began to cry and put his head onto his father's shoulder. Roza moved over to both of them, and they all embraced. As a unit, their little family was always together and she had this nagging dread that she was going to lose everything. She cried into Ser's shoulders, closed her eyes, and drank in his scent. The darkness and the feeling of his muscular shoulder reminded her of the vast, silent mountains around Kobane. She savored this momentary comfort and imagined none of this was happening. But that couldn't last. He pulled back.

"I love you, Sweet," she said quietly. "May *Xwa* keep you safe. Please be careful."

"I love you, Roz. *Xwa* be with you, too." Sercan touched her cheek. They kissed gently. She didn't want to let go.

Sercan turned to Yez. "Remember, my little lion, I love you. I'm fighting for you and your Mama."

"Yes, Papa, love you…" He looked down.

Sercan would be picked up by other men who were fighting, including Karin's brother Ahman. At least they would be together. Roza couldn't bear the pain in her chest. It felt as if her heart was being constricted and she couldn't breathe. However, she had to keep going. Hatred towards Daesh was building inside her, for what they were doing to her people, and now to her family. *We will never surrender*. But she felt sick knowing that Sercan could die.

***

Two-and-a-half weeks later, Roza was cleaning metal plates in her kitchen. She and Yez had been living in Kobane under survival conditions with the other residents. She had had contact with Sercan while he was on the frontline. Daesh was upon them, with tanks and artillery, and the Kurdish civilians did not have the weaponry to fight back. It was becoming terrifying now, and Roza worried every moment of the day for Sercan. Karin came and knocked on her door.

"Rozi."

"Hello, Kar. What's happening?"

"I need to talk to you."

"Okay, just a minute…is something wrong?" Roza dried her hands with the towel, searching Karin's face.

"It's Sercan…he was fighting under heavy enemy attack. The wall he was shooting through was completely destroyed by artillery fire…I'm so sorry, Roz. He didn't make it…" Karin broke down and moved towards Roza.

"What?" Roza said, a shrill sound escaping. Karin's words seemed to reach Roza in slow motion as if they were in an alternative reality. Not the one where she lived with her husband raising their child. She couldn't comprehend the words; he couldn't be gone…

"Rozi, I'm so sorry."

"What do you mean?"

"He was injured by shrapnel and parts of the wall fell on him. They tried to revive him… but…"

"What? No…that can't be right."

Roza felt as if her legs were giving way. She fell backward onto the wall, sliding down she sobbed uncontrollably.

"I can't breathe, Kar, I can't breathe…"

Karin moved towards her and embraced her tightly on the floor. Roza's body was limp as if it was losing its strength, seeping out through the pores of her skin.

"Will I see him? Will I be able to have his body?"

"I'm sorry, Rozi. They'll give him a traditional burial in the graveyard over there. They can't move him over here; it's too dangerous. The men are devastated too. It's too dangerous for you to go over there. I wanted to tell you, Roz—you know I'm joining the resistance, don't you?"

"Yes, Kar. I always knew you would."

"I'm leaving tomorrow. I'm so sorry I can't be here longer, for you. I want to be, but I had arranged it a few days ago. I want you to know I will avenge Ser's death. He was like another brother to me. Daesh will pay. I know how much Ser loved you and you him. I'll fight for him and Mani. Their deaths," Karin broke down, then continued, "will not be for nothing."

"Thanks, Kar, that means a lot to me." She hugged Karin. "Please come and see me later before you go, but now I have to tell Yez."

Roza ran to find Yez. She found him outside, and embraced him weeping.

"Your daddy became a martyr today," she told him. "He gave his life for us." She could barely say the words; they seemed hollow. They embraced in the dirt of the street. Yez and Roza began to sob loudly, and they were one, joined together by this unbearable pain. It was as if they were the only people left in the world.

***

Roza found out what details she could about Sercan's last moments. From reports, he had been firing from the cover of a wall when it was blown up by enemy fire. She kept asking details from Yusef Ser's close friend, and he finally admitted that Ser's body was shredded by shrapnel—shards of pottery and bricks—

and covered in blood. Roza gasped and began to weep when she heard. Yusef said he had cleaned and covered his body. His face was decimated and unrecognizable. Medics had been called, those who had stayed in Kobane, but when they arrived, he had died. When she heard this, she dropped the phone and wept, cold, bitter tears. She could not stop pacing around weeping, touching her forehead with the palm of her hand. Darkness descended upon her frame. She craved the touch of Sercan and embraced herself, feeling empty with the absence of his arms. As she stood in the middle of the dusty white road, Yez came and touched her arm.

"Mama," he said, in a tone that pleaded with her. "Are you okay?"

Roza looked down at Yez, his perfect dark eyes that reflected his father. There was this way Sercan asked a question, with humility in his voice, as if you knew more than him. She forced herself to smile, pulled him close to herself, and said nothing. Then, in mechanical fashion, she went back to their house and set about getting him the eggs they had obtained from a family nearby.

In the nights that followed, Roza became withdrawn, and barely spoke. It was difficult to sleep; they could hear the distant sound of mortar fire and explosions. Every night, Yez cried himself to sleep and woke up screaming his father's name. Roza had to calm him down and put cold cloths on his face. The grief settled into quietness but remained between them as a bond. Roza found it easy to obey Islamic instruction about grieving; four months and ten days of mourning, wearing no adornments or jewelry, and as for marrying again, this was out of the question. In the past ten days, Turkey had closed the border for anyone wanting to come in. Now, even if they wanted to leave, they were trapped in Kobane.

"Ser, I don't think I can do this," Roza spoke into the corner of the dark room as she sat on her cushion. "I can't stay here and do nothing."

"Roza." Naze came to the door of her daughter's room, "Is everything okay? I heard speaking. I thought someone was here."

Roza laughed a little. "It was me…talking to Sercan." She smiled at her mother. Naze entered the room and sat crossed legged arranging her long skirt around herself on the mat. She looked at Roza with concern.

"I'm worried about you, Rozi. You seem a bit…"

"What?" Roza said as she felt her cheeks become warm.

"I don't know. You don't interact with Yez much, and he's worried about you. He doesn't say it, but I know he is."

"I'm okay, but I don't know if I can do this."

"What?"

"Stay here and wait for all of us to be killed. Now that the border is closed, we're trapped. I thought we could leave, but now that's not an option. Ser's blood is in the dirt crying out to me, and I just lie here every day."

"I know, Roz, but you're Yez's mother, he needs you."

"I know… but what he really needs is to be defended. What kind of a mother am I if I let Daesh kill him? I don't want to wait here for them to come to us."

"We'll be okay," Naze said.

"We're in danger here, and I don't want Ser's death to be for nothing."

"I know what you're saying."

"Sorry, Ma but I have no choice. I don't want you or Dad killed either."

Naze did not say anything. Roza could see that she was deep in thought and distressed.

"Leaving will kill me, but…I need to defend Yez from a brutal death. I'm not waiting here to be captured or killed. I think you know I'm right, Ma. Do you understand? I won't be a good mother if I do nothing."

"I don't know. Wouldn't Sercan want you to stay with Yez?"

"Ser would want me to protect Yez."

Naze paused, and, after a few moments, she seemed resigned to what her daughter was saying. She didn't speak.

"I know I will hate leaving Yez. Of course, I will. But I have to defend him, his father, and our land. Otherwise, what future does Yez have? Daesh will win. We're stuck here now. Besides, I can come back and see Yez after a little bit."

"That's true," Naze said.

"You've always told me Ocalan would want us to fight."

Naze looked into Roza's eyes.

"I don't want you to enlist, but I understand what you're saying. I don't want to lose you. I don't think I can talk about this right now. It's too difficult."

"Okay, we can talk later. I love you, Ma. It's not a choice I want to make, but I feel there is no choice now. You know I wouldn't do this if I didn't have to."

"I know, sweetheart. I love you too." Naze touched Roza's shoulder as she left the room. Roza sat in silence. She saw Sercan sitting near her, blood all over his face, mutilated by the shrapnel and concrete that had lacerated his face and chest. He was sitting there, with arms outstretched, hands open and upward-facing. His face was contorted in pain, with dark crimson oozing out of his torso and soaking into his clothes.

Roza fell onto her bed; she didn't know how she would be able to say goodbye to Yez. Inside there was a conviction solidifying in her stomach of what she had to do. Karin had already joined the resistance, and now Roza couldn't stop thinking about it. Every morning, it was all she thought about. It was as if she had died with Sercan, and no longer felt anything. All she felt was a burning desire to make Daesh pay for taking everything from her. How could she leave Yez though? With the border closed as of a few days ago, Roza felt more desperate. They were trapped, and now she had no choice but to defend Yez and their homeland. As the days passed, Roza's insides felt like fire, burning up and consuming the softer parts of herself. She felt as if doing nothing was insulting to Ser and what he had started. What kind of a mother would not defend her son but just let them come and kill all of them? One morning, Roza woke up and knew she had to act. She contacted Karin and arranged to join the YPJ. She wondered whether there were rules about a mourning woman fighting a war against those who also claimed to be Muslim, but she dismissed the thought. From the moment Ser was killed, something had changed within her. Her future had become darkened by a threatening cloud, that felt like it would envelop her at any moment and destroy everything she loved. She felt fearful of Yez's future and her own, and wouldn't let them take Yez, or the land they had fought strenuously to gain. What future did he have if they lost their homeland? Years of waiting in some refugee camp for a country to accept them, in lines of white tents shrouded by uncertainty and desperation? And then they would be far, far from Kobane, from *their* place, from Sercan and from who they were. She would not let this happen. When it was safe again, everyone would return, and they would know it was because she and her comrades never surrendered to Daesh.

Yez had sobbed when she left. Roza felt like she would vomit, but she had to go, and hoped he understood. She had told him she would try to see him when she could, during the battle, and remembered watching his tiny body recede as she sat on the back of the truck that drove away. He had watched her leaving intently and held his hand in the victory sign to the sky. He looked like he was trying to be brave.

Naze stood next to him, hugging him. Roza's chest tightened, and her stomach churned. Her insides felt like they were being constricted and twisted. Who was she? She didn't know anymore. It was as if a mechanized being had replaced who she was, but it helped to be devoid of emotion. If she allowed her

53

feelings to flow, Roza felt she might die from its flooding. Now, she wanted to act. She blew Yez a kiss and prayed for the day she could return to him. If all went well, *Xwa* willing, she may be reunited with him very soon. She hoped so.

- 5 -

Karin

Camp Berivan,

Mid October, 2014

It was a crisp morning when Karin left Maia and Aster, as the sun rose above the hills surrounding Kobane. She was driving with the other volunteers across town to a place far enough outside the combat that they could do their training. Karin was a little nervous passing through the desolate town that was once bustling, but she just kept thinking about Mani.

After a thirty-minute drive, Karin and her other comrades reached Camp Berivan, which was outside of Kobane. It was some kilometers away from where Daesh was, and had been set up for the training of recruits for the fight. When Karin walked into the two-story building there, she was surprised by the pink walls inside. The brightly colored paint was patchy, and the wallpaper was peeling off in large sections, it looked like it could have been a beauty parlor or school. Her fellow comrades greeted her. A woman came up to Karin and was the first to greet her properly. She kissed Karin four times on the cheek as was customary.

"Welcome, comrade. Come in."

"Thank you," Karin answered, entering the main room.

"I'm Tanah. What's your name?" Tanah was tall, solid and quietly spoken.

"Karin."

Tanah's hair was tied up under her khaki cap, and she smiled a small and gentle smile. Karin felt instantly calm around her; she seemed peaceful and kind.

"Good to meet you, Karin," Tanah said, as she introduced two girls standing next to her, they were Reynaz and Torani. Torani wouldn't look into Karin's eyes; she was only sixteen and timid. Torani radiated cheekiness and seemed like she had a wicked side, someone who enjoyed making people laugh. She could tell by the way the other women teased her in a good-natured way; there was a humor that surrounded her. She seemed like one of those people you felt was about to make light of the situation. She felt instantly motherly towards Torani, and that was unusual for her as she had never felt this toward anyone. Karin had not wanted domestic life in the sense of being a mother and wife, though she had once entertained the idea, with her fiancée at the time, Terah. Briefly, her thoughts turned to him. She wondered if he was safe in Iraq, where he was fighting.

When they had gone inside and sat down, Karin and Torani began to talk. She told Karin that she came from Cizre, Turkey; her mother had wanted to marry her off recently. She said her mother mustn't have loved her as she wanted to force her to do something she didn't want to do. So, Torani began to skip school and go to be with the YPJ supporters. With her comrades, Torani would watch Daesh videos of beheadings and women

56

being dragged behind cars by their hair. Seeing people executed on the banks of the river or in ditches, shot down like animals, Torani was enraged and disturbed. She swore that would never let this happen to her friends or family. One day, on a public holiday, she planned her escape. She packed a small bag, told her father to take care, and left. He didn't know she was leaving; she didn't say goodbye to any of her family. None of her friends knew she had joined the YPJ either. Torani had a smile on her face, but also tears around the corners of her eyes, as if a storm threatened to fall at any moment. It was not an easy choice to make at the age of sixteen. Karin could see in her bravado, how she wanted to appear strong.

There had been nearly a hundred of them crossing the Turkish border on the day they were shot at while they ran across the expanse. Some of them were injured, and one of their friends was killed. Torani had told Karin with a smirk, "I just ran, looked ahead, and kept running."

Karin touched her on the arm. "May *Xwa* be with you always," she said. She hugged Torani, which was surprising for both of them. She wasn't normally this affectionate. It was a little awkward afterward, but they both laughed and moved into the larger group. Tanah seemed to be someone who didn't waste her words, Karin noticed, as she watched her talk to the others. *These are my new people, my new family*, Karin thought as she looked at the faces in the room. Getting up from her seated position, she felt a dull sadness. Though Karin felt a lump in her throat, she suppressed it. She walked out onto the concrete veranda and lit up a cigarette from the tobacco her father had given her. She touched the leather band on her wrist and thought of Aster and Mani. She hoped they were safe. At least where they were was away from the fighting. She thought of Roza and wished she could talk to her. It was possible at some point that she could ring Roza. They were able to make contact on mobile phones when they sometimes had coverage.

Exhaling into the air, she began to relax, especially when she heard the sound of laughter from the other room. These women were warm and accepting. Y*es, this can be my home.* Some of the women came outside to see Karin and walked out into the expansive courtyard. Karin wondered what they were going to do. She followed them onto the dirt-filled expanse. Torani, Tanah, and Reynaz were stretching out a rope. Reynaz and Tanah took their positions. Torani jumped in a jerky fashion over the rope.

"Aren't your shoes going to fall off?" Tanah called to Torani.

Torani didn't answer; she simply flung the slipping shoes off her feet and kept jumping in her socks. They all began to laugh, including Karin.

"Are you going to join in?" Tanah asked Karin.

"No, I'm happy watching," Karin said, smiling. "You're very entertaining."

Torani laughed and continued to jump, flinging her legs with abandon. Karin began to feel that she was not an outsider anymore. She was grateful it had not taken too long to feel included. She had noticed men had been coming into the compound all day, and now noticed some other young men and women playing a game of soccer together. One young man asked

Karin to join, and she accepted, relieved to be able to release her nervous energy. She was told she would meet the Commander soon. Karin couldn't help but be impressed with how these men and women were freely interacting as friends. This did not happen back at home. She truly felt part of a revolution, running with the ball and jostling with the men for it.

These small actions showed Karin that, ironically within the training camp, a revolution was occurring. Though Daesh wanted to take women back into the dark ages, here the Kurdish forces were quietly achieving social change to take back to their society. Things were changing, even if in small increments. Karin enjoyed jostling for the ball and eventually got down the end and scored in the makeshift goal. She threw her arms up, and clicked her tongue in high-pitched celebration, running around in a circle. The other girls embraced her. It felt exhilarating to play like this.

***

After the soccer game, Karin sat down on her own on the wall, smoking. She was thinking about her parents and Roza, wondering if they were safe. A young girl came over to her and introduced herself as Amara. *She couldn't be any older than sixteen.* She had long dark hair pulled into a ponytail that fell onto her back, dark eyes, and eyebrows that were fine and thin. Below her cheekbones, she had pronounced dimples when she smiled. Karin felt impressed that Amara had given up her teenage life to fight.

"*Silav*, Amara."

"*Silav.*"

"How did you get to become part of the YPJ?"

"I came with my family's blessing. My brothers and father are a part of the YPG. When I asked my mother if I could come, she simply answered—who can say no to such an honor? She knew it was an honor to serve our people like this, to fight for our land and culture."

"That's amazing," Karin said. "My family were hesitant. I had to leave without them fully blessing it."

"That's understandable, isn't it? People don't understand how we could do it."

"Yes, true."

Karin was amazed at how mature this girl was, she seemed to have the mind of a 30-year-old. When Karin looked around at the girls who were there, she was somewhat taken aback at how young they were. They barely looked as if they had finished high school. There were some women her age, in their twenties, but the majority of the women were probably sixteen to twenty years old. Karin still missed Roza and wondered how she was coping with the grief about Sercan. She had wanted to be there for her closest friend, but what she could do? Now, she would fight for Mani and Sercan and her family, as she promised Roza she would.

"Let's introduce you to the Commander," Amara said, guiding Karin over to the group of women standing in the compound talking. She smiled at the Commander, who then came towards them.

"Welcome, Karin. I'm Commander Tolhedan." They kissed each other and said hello. Karin was surprised that she felt nervous.

"I have heard of the sacrifice your brother made. May he rest in peace. He was brave and strong. I'm sorry for your loss."

"Thank you," Karin said, feeling her cheeks warm. The Commander had a sensitivity around her eyes and seemed softer than Karin imagined. Karin had envisaged a tough-minded, harsh military leader. Tolhedan seemed like an aunty of Karin's, smiling with warmth and sharing jokes with the girls.

"I see you have met Amara, very good," Tolhedan said. "We'll be having a brief meeting on the veranda. I look forward to getting to know you, Karin."

"Thank you very much, Commander."

The Commander walked across the dusty expanse to where some of the girls were already sitting. She sat down crossed-legged in front of the girls and began to speak. Karin followed and sat down as well.

"First of all, I hope you have met Karin and made her welcome. She arrived today."

Many of the girls nodded and smiled toward her. She smiled shyly back at the group wanting everything to move on. The Commander then began to speak.

"Freedom crowns the heads of the free, but only slaves know its value. In our society, being a wife or a daughter means you are not a person in your own right. And, if you're a man, you belong to the system. Every master has a master of its own. A woman toils all day in the kitchen, bears and raises kids, but it's like she is not there. People say, 'She is just a woman.' There's a saying in our society, 'A woman is a broken tree.' But we say, no! A woman can fight! A woman can do it. But what kind of woman? Only a woman who knows herself."

Karin was enraptured by what she was saying. She had read Ocalan talking about the rights of women, but now, right here, it seemed to be so much more real.

"What does that mean? A woman who knows where she's from and what she is becoming now and her role. Your role is now as a soldier. Being a soldier is a struggle with yourself. That's why I will ask you: what's a soldier's life to you?" The Commander said, examining the girls' faces.

Karin could see many of the girls looked down. Who would answer? Normally Karin would, but she was new here.

"Comrade Aza?"

"A soldier must watch their words."

"Yes, watch their words, and Comrade Amara?"

"Consistency and discipline," Amara answered.

Another girl Karin hadn't met said, "If a soldier isn't focused in life, they won't focus in war."

"Soldiers must estrange themselves from society." Commander Tolhedan said, nodding.

One girl from down the middle of the room said, "A soldier must be attached to their homeland."

"A soldier must be cold-hearted in battle," another girl from the other side of the room called out.

Karin put up her hand and said, "May I?" She laughed a little. "A soldier must not keep quiet." The Commander looked at her and smiled.

"War brings great destruction. A peaceful country is not like a country at war, where you hear explosions every day; people get wounded and killed. Either we will perish or become soldiers. There are no other alternatives," she said. The women's faces looked serious, and Karin looked down at her lap, picking pieces of lint off her pants.

"Each of you should ask yourselves: how long will I last? If an enemy comes, will I be able to load my gun and pull the trigger? Can I do it?"

Tolhedan paused. She looked at them all and then said, "It's something you all need to think about. Does anyone have any questions?" No one stirred. In a more light-hearted tone, she said, "Something to think about, girls. Let's have some lunch. Come." They all rose to their feet and began to walk to the kitchen or out into the courtyard.

Karin questioned herself. Was she ready? After all this time, wanting to join the armed forces for her people, was she really ready to be a soldier? She decided to have a cigarette. Sitting down on the fence, she rolled one. Some of the girls began to kick the ball. There was a lot to consider. Tanah approached

Karin and said she had her uniform and weaponry ready. Karin went with Tanah into the building, feeling keen to receive her military gear. It might help with her reservations and slight nerves, though she didn't want to show it to the others. She still wore Mani's khaki pants, held up with a piece of rope because they were too big. She laughed a little when she put them on in the morning, knowing that Mani would think they looked ridiculous on her.

***

"Torani, get up, sleepy head," Tanah said. Karin could hear a commotion in the room where they slept. Torani often slept in. The girls were laughing loudly; at least she provided some comic relief.

"Leave me alone, please leave me alone!" she cried, curling up under her blanket. *Typical teenager*, Karin remembered how Ahman was always sleeping in when he was in his mid-teens. Tanah began spraying a water bottle onto Torani, as she rose out of bed.

"Leave me alone, am I a toy to you? I don't even get left alone in the toilet," Torani said, laughing. Standing up, her hair was a matted mess on her head. Torani always wore a bright rainbow-colored jacket. It suited her personality. The girls began to laugh as well, and Karin joined in with all of them. What would they do without Torani? She looked at her watch and realized they had to go to their class with the Commander. They walked across the compound and entered the dimly-lit room, and saw the Commander holding a gun as some of the girls sat up against the walls, watching intently. Karin sat down, as did Torani and Tanah.

"This is a Russian-made gun. It is a *Kalashnikov*. It can fire a single bullet or several bullets at a time." She was holding the gun upright, showing them where the holster and magazine opened up and how the bullets were fitted. Then she pointed it down and said, "Keep your finger here until you find the target." She pointed to the area near the trigger and paused over it. "As you aim, control your breathing, like we've practiced. A millimeter may make a big difference when you are aiming at the target. Right, who wants to load the gun blindfolded?"

"Me, me, I can!" Torani called.

The Commander agreed, smiling. Torani was always the first to get involved. Commander Tolhedan put a scarf over her eyes and gave her a magazine in which to load the bullets. Torani held the gun and began to put rounds into the magazine; however, they were not going in correctly. The girls started to laugh as she looked quite comical. She began to try to attach the magazine to what she thought was the gun clip. She could not quite do it. The girls were calling out, "It's upside down."

"What do you mean upside down?" She continued to seek to push the magazine. The Commander came over and took off her blindfold.

"You have the gun upside down. You can't get the magazine in. Let's take a break." She laughed a little. Torani looked down at the gun.

"Ah, there it is," she said, clicking the magazine into its correct place. The girls began to walk out into the other room, some of them laughing amongst themselves. Karin walked past and patted her on the shoulder.

"Good try, comrade."

"*Zor spas*." Torani looked up and smiled.

- 6 -

Roza

Camp Berivan

Late October, 2014

R oza sat on the back of the utility vehicle with tears blurring her vision the whole way to the training camp. She had crossed Kobane the same route as Karin, scared in case Daesh was lurking behind every building. Now, on the back of the Toyota Hilux, she was being transported with other women to the training camp. It was horrible to be going through Kobane and seeing the devastation. Her stomach felt tight. She thought of Sercan as she passed through her home town and wondered what his last moments were like. Did he think of her? Yez came into her mind as well. She tried not to picture him standing there with her mother. She had to put him out of her mind.

When she arrived at the training camp, which was three kilometers from the frontline in Kobane, two women came to greet her. One was a well-built woman with a wide white smile, dark, long curly hair, and a khaki bandana on her head. Her name was Tanah. She greeted Roza with the customary four kisses, one on either side then two on the same cheek. Another lady came to Roza and welcomed her; Reynaz, a slim younger woman with short dark hair and a pointed nose. Reynaz seemed self-assured and grounded. Roza had not seen Karin yet. Where was she? She walked into the building's lounge room, where she stood and leaned on the wall. Tears began to form in her eyes, and she felt utterly alone. Had she done the right thing? What was she doing here? Why did she leave Yez for this? What the hell was she doing? She stood there, her emotions overtaking her fine features.

One of the women called out to her, "Are you okay?" It was a girl who looked to Roza to be very young. She was short, and her body was slim. She smirked when she smiled, as if she was going to tell you something funny. She kissed Roza hello, stood back, examined her face, and then said her name was Torani.

"You'll be okay, lady. We're all in this together. We've all left family. For me though, my mother didn't love me, so that's different. But let's not talk about that." The girl laughed nervously.

"I'm sure your mother loves you," Roza blurted out, the mention of motherhood was like a knife in her chest.

"I don't think so. She wanted to marry me off to an old man. I'm sixteen. I told her I would not, but she was still going ahead with it. What kind of mother does that?" She looked at Roza; her face reflected pain mixed with seeking to be brave and light-hearted. She couldn't hide how she felt from Roza.

"Maybe she's a mother stuck in the old way of thinking. Maybe she thinks it'll be best for you. I can tell you one thing though; she loves you. I'm sure of it."

"Thank you. Welcome to our world now. Here we can actually fight for our rights, and you'll find you get more respect with a gun over your shoulder than you have ever had. It's intense but worth it." She smiled at Roza and then walked out of the room.

"Rozi!" Karin called to her in a high-pitched voice as she entered the room. Roza had never seen Karin like this, all animated; she was normally so reserved. They embraced, and Roza didn't let go for quite a few moments.

"How was Yez when you left?" Karin looked into Roza's face.

"He was okay, Kar. It was extremely difficult. But I can't just wait until Daesh comes to get us. I hope Yez understood this." Roza's voice was shaky.

Karin touched her arm. "Yes, I think he understands. He knows you're doing this to protect him, honor Ser, and stop them from destroying Kobane."

"Thanks, Kar. I think he did." Roza looked away.

"Have you met some of the women? They're very nice," Karin said, changing the subject.

"Yes, I've met a few."

"Let's get you some tea and something to eat." Karin took Roza into the kitchen, where she put the pot onto the woodfire stove, and they sat together on the cushions on the floor. A large picture was hanging on the wall. Roza asked Karin who it was.

"That's Berivan. This camp is named after her; she was a great martyr."

"I see."

"These camps have to move around constantly, though. I'm sure you were told that by our YPJ comrades."

"Yes, I was."

***

The next morning, as the sun rose, the girls were lined up ten in a row, and the Commander motioned to them to do their exercises. They touched their toes, their chest, and then pointed to the sky in unison. One, two, three, one, two, three. Some had not been given their uniform yet and still wore their normal clothes. Karin was standing next to Roza, and she was wearing her uniform, all in khaki. She looked professional doing the exercises. After this, they were asked to jog around the compound. Some of the girls waited for Commander Tolhedan, and some of them began to kick a soccer ball. One girl had a skipping rope and began to jump rope with precision and skill. This town had been abandoned by the villagers, and the camp was in various buildings. There was a dog left behind. He had dirt all over his patchy white fur, and limped on his right hind leg. But he still had a crazy, welcoming smile and manner that only a dog could have in this situation.

Roza had become emotional when she saw the dirty mattresses on the floor. She had cried herself to sleep for the first few nights, feeling as if she couldn't breathe on the musty mattress. She made sure she was silent, though. On the outside of the building was a child's dust-covered, rusted bike, leaning up against a completely rusted bathing tub. It made her feel sick when she saw reminders of Yez or childhood or domesticity. This was what she had to push down now; she had to move away from this. If she was to be a good soldier, these things could not cause her to falter now. She thought of Sercan and pictured his face. Just then Torani came to Roza and presented her with the khakis, then walked away. Roza looked at the items of clothing and went into the room where they slept. The dog was lying on the concrete floor. He looked up at her and then put his head down again. She began to undress and put her clothes on the floor—her blue shirt with flowers, her jeans. She picked up the khaki pants and put her legs into the fabric's heavy bagginess. They were a bit big for her; she would have to get a belt. Keeping her t-shirt on and the purple scarf that Sercan had given her, she protected herself from the cold air that was arriving during the days now. Putting the khaki shirt over her shoulder, she traced the edges of the YPJ green triangle with the red star in the middle of her arm. Buttoning it up, she told herself, *This is the new you, Rozi.* The old is gone now.

To keep warm, she put her navy-blue jacket back on over the shirt. Finally, she had all the gear on. She tenderly touched her purple scarf, kissed it, and thought of Sercan again. She vowed she would always keep him close.

"You ready?" Karin peered through the door.

"Yep." She walked out into the half overcast and half sun-lit day. They moved to another building with a large veranda where all the women and girls sat against the wall.

Commander Tolhedan stood in front of them. "There are some new recruits to our group. Welcome ladies. I am Commander

Tolhedan, and I've been working with the YPJ for four years now. I train new recruits. That's my job." She smiled at all of them.

Roza thought what a kind and soft face she had. Her skin looked smooth, and her face reflected perfect symmetry in her high cheekbones and a nose that was just the right size and proportion. She had faint lines around her eyes and her lips were perfectly shaped as if someone had drawn them expertly on her face. Roza felt she radiated beauty from her physical features, but also gentleness. Around her neck, she had a brightly colored scarf with floral decorations in green and red. She was bright and easy to listen to. Roza felt it was because she had trained so many women.

Two ginger-and-white cats wandered past the group, and Roza wondered how they managed to survive, and not only that, but look so clean and healthy. One of them stopped and began to groom himself, licking his front paw. In all this devastation of humanity, these cats seemed to be thriving. Roza smiled and admired this about them. It was a touch of their old life walking amongst them, a hope that things would not always be like this.

Roza hadn't noticed, but men started to file into the compound. The girls were motioned to stand, and they all did against the wall. The men filed onto the veranda and began shaking the hands of all the women, moving along the line. Roza shook their hands as they went, looking down. It was a bit uncomfortable. Then they sat alongside the women as well, propping weaponry up next to them and facing the Commander.

"The Islamic State has mapped out the country it's trying to create. Look at its borders and regions it attacks, and you will see Kurdistan, comrades. There's always danger. Don't think it will be like this all the time. Tomorrow, everything could turn against us. Our strength, courage, determination, organization, and knowledge of the enemy will save us. That's all for today. Any questions? I will also talk to people individually, and some of you need to be equipped before we do some more physical training. *Zor spas*, everyone."

The recruits all looked around at each other. They began to stand and chanted "Free Kurdistan!" as they moved out. Some of the women wrapped scarves around their necks as the men began to disperse as well. Roza did not know what to do. The Commander came directly to Roza and squatted in front of her.

"Come, Roza, we have to equip you." She stood up, took Roza by the hand, and Karin rose as well. They went into the room off the veranda. She picked up a vest, and putting it around Roza's shoulders, said, "There's a grenade in there, right?" Roza nodded, putting it carefully on.

"This is your weapon," she said, handing Roza an AK47. Roza held it awkwardly, feeling its weight and bulkiness for the first time.

"Right, we will be doing some drills soon. Come out into the courtyard, when you're comfortable."

Roza and Karin nodded and followed the Commander out into the dusty courtyard where there were about twenty women lined up. They began to run in a circle, then came back to the line and stood to attention holding their weapons down.

"Hold your weapons tighter," Tolhedan called out. Roza and Karin joined the line. Karin was better at the drill, as she had been there for two weeks and was well practiced already.

"If a fly flies onto your face or your hair falls onto your face, you can't touch it, okay? You must stand upright like now, chest forward and looking ahead. At ease. Attention!" She called out, and the girls responded to her commands by placing their feet apart and then together and pointing their guns out and up. Roza tried to be in sync but was struggling in the line behind the front row. The Commander tested all of the women individually, calling their names in pairs. It came to Roza and Karin. Roza tried to keep up with Karin's pace. The Commander simply smiled and moved onto the next pair.

"Turn left!" All of the women turned to their left, except one woman turned to her right and ended up facing the other women. They began to laugh. "Girls, I said turn left!" called the Commander. The woman facing the wrong way, turned herself the correct way, blushing. Then she said it again, "Turn left" and more of the women turned in different directions. They were now facing each other.

"Where is your direction, comrades?" All of the women began to laugh and point at each other. Even the Commander began to laugh. Roza and Karin had got it right, but they joined in. It was like a brief shower of rain on a sun-drenched day. Roza wondered how these women, including herself, would ever be able to become soldiers and kill people. A strong bond had been formed between the women and the Commander Roza noticed.

"Don't worry, girls, you're doing well. We'll get there. You have left everything for this, and I respect you." Roza looked at Karin, smiling; the others also seemed more relaxed. It was obvious these women had already become close, as some of them had been there a few weeks. One of the girls at the front dropped her weapon, and Roza looked down not wanting to embarrass her. *She may be new like me.* Then the Commander dismissed them and told them to relax for a little bit. Some of the women began to dance and sing, and Roza and Karin sat watching them. Torani, Tanah, and Reynaz sang while kicking their legs side to side. Then they sat inside the circle as well. The women began to sing in Kurdish, and Roza joined in. Singing relieved her nerves and calmed her, especially in her mother tongue, forbidden for so many years.

The hour of the Kurds has come,

We will end the injustice!

The YPJ weapons will make Rojava a peaceful place…

Clapping as they sang, the women made high-pitched reverberating noises, clicking their tongues at the end of the verses. This call, Roza knew, caused anxiety in Daesh when they heard it after the decree was made that 'anyone killed by a woman would go to hell.' They all began to laugh again. Roza liked this feeling of being part of something larger; she put thoughts of Yez aside right now. She had a mission, and she would complete it.

The women began to sing another song. Roza recognized it and knew the words.

Enough, mother!

I want to be a revolutionary.

All of my friends are there.

I'm the only one,

Shamefully staying on the side lines,

I don't feel right here.

My soul cries out for the mountains.

Mother, please don't cry.

Then the women trailed off and began to laugh. These words echoed in Roza's head; this was exactly how she felt. It was a feeling of belonging. She had found women with the same desire she had, to do something. Roza looked around the group of women and was relieved that her nerves about joining the YPJ had dissipated. These were simply women like herself, wanting the same thing. One of them stood up, noticing the men were playing a game of soccer, and she motioned for the girls to follow. They all moved towards the young men who had started to kick the ball around. Roza and Karin followed. Karin joined in, inviting Roza to as well.

"I'll just watch from here, for now," Roza answered.

Watching them all tackle and barge for the ball, running around, they all seemed without a care in the world. Who would know from looking at this picture that within a few kilometers, Daesh was lurking, seeking to overtake and destroy them? But here, Roza looked up at the sky, seeing it was blue, with only a few clouds and even the sound of birds in the distance. Here, she could fool herself into thinking this was normal life, though it wasn't *their* normal. Karin tripped over the ball and looked up at Roza, laughing. Roza laughed too, and felt that just as they were changing into soldiers, the world of the Kurds was changing from within. *Our revolution is starting, and I won't surrender it to anyone.* Finally, Roza decided to join in. She ran into the game and began to chase the ball, kicking it out of the group and moving it towards the goal. For the first time in months, Roza felt free.

- 7 -

Karin

Every morning they rose early to do drills, jogging around the compound, learning to take commands as a squadron. Karin was getting into the rhythm of it. She had learned how to hold her gun so that it didn't dig in as she ran, or didn't swing too far around her body. This morning, there was word that Roza was coming. She couldn't believe it. Rozi here? It was hard to imagine Rozi, an English literature teacher, gentle friend, and mother, joining the fight. Karin didn't know what to think about the fact that she was leaving Yez.

If Roza had made this decision, then she must have felt strongly about it. Karin understood that feeling. Who was she to judge Rozi? She had known Rozi her whole life, and trusted her completely, knew her gentleness and kindness as well her sense of fun. Karin remembered their wanderings and the play of childhood and adolescence, how Rozi would laugh at the men who were pursuing her or Karin. Roza had long, wavy, dark hair, and eyebrows shaped like someone had expertly drawn them with a pencil. Her cheekbones were finely formed, like a marble sculpture, but her eyes, Karin felt, were where she reflected herself. The easy-going, light, and spirited woman looked through those deep brown eyes. Now, though, Karin knew everything was different, and so was she.

Roza had lost Sercan. Karin didn't know if Roza would ever recover. From the moment she and Sercan met, Karin had seen their connection, from the nervous laughter and to the eyes glancing to and from each other. Roza was sometimes standoffish around men. Karin had to admit she was jealous when they first got together. Sercan was a kind and good-natured man, but Karin missed Rozi. She felt she didn't see her anymore. In time, Karin realized Sercan was a loyal and supportive man. Rozi deserved this after her tumultuous childhood. Karin came to accept them as a couple and even began to really like him. She was devastated when he was killed. She had told Rozi straight away; it *had* to come from her, not someone else. Rozi could barely speak. What did Karin expect? She had wanted Rozi to know she would fight for Sercan as much as for Mani. And now, Roza was joining the fight as well. Karin had no idea, at that point, that she would join.

Did either of them know what they were doing? How could they? It was impossible to imagine, but soon, within a few weeks, they would be on the frontline. No turning back then. Karin did not want to turn back; she kept reminding herself of the barbarity of Daesh. They had beheaded Mani and tried to take his dignity and humanity, but they had failed. He would always be her funny and clumsy brother, that she loved more than life.

Karin had asked the Commander yesterday what it was like on the frontline. Tolhedan had told her she'd fought at

Serekaniyi; that was where she was born. She said she had been face-to-face with the enemy.

"You simply had to fire and hope you hit them first," the older woman said. "They were firing, and you were firing, and someone would come out in the end. It's very close range. Just remember, it will be like nothing you've ever been through. There are not many things that can prepare you for it. Two people facing each other, firing. Killing the enemy close up. You will be able to see his eyes before he dies, and you need to prepare somehow for this. I'm not saying I know how you can prepare, except that I wish to warn you of what it's like."

"I've heard some things about you in battle. That you won a battle…but I don't know the details."

"There was one battle where we were stationed on an outcrop hill overlooking Serekaniyi. I was firing my weapon down to Daesh positions below. We had grenade launchers and guns, and I was constantly firing. Then, this almighty explosion happened right near me. My friends only saw white smoke and dust, and they thought I was dead. For some miraculous reason, I was not harmed. After the dust settled, I stood up–they had all been waiting with anticipation, and then there I was, unharmed. We won that battle, and they called that point 'Tolhedan Point' after me, which was very nice. I couldn't believe it."

"That's amazing," Karin felt awed by this woman. Tolhedan stood up and gently touched Karin on the arm and then left. Karin sat on the veranda deep in thought, watching the pink and yellow sunset, and looking longingly to the mountain range surrounding Kobane. She wished they could all flee into the mountains, live simply in the caves and hills as their ancestors had, the ancient Kurds, also known as the Medes. If only, Karin thought.

***

Roza was arriving today, and Karin was excited. When she saw her, she had already met a lot of the other women. She looked overwhelmed but pleased to see Karin. They hugged so tightly that Karin felt as if she would lose her breath. *Obviously, Roza has been through a lot.* They would be okay if they got through this together, just like they had with everything else in their lives; puberty, periods, boys, violence, university, parental and societal expectations of women, and much more. When Roza got married, their paths diverged somewhat, but their bond remained the same and Karin loved Yez as her own. He had so much of Roza in him.

"How was Yez when you left?" Karin saw sadness darken Roza's face in a way she had never seen before. Roza looked different somehow, but grief does this to you. Her shoulders seemed smaller and bonier; ironic given her new status in the fight against an enemy as merciless as Daesh. If Karin could think of a word to describe how she looked, it would be 'harrowed,' as if she had seen some hellish apparition and was now, forever altered.

"He was okay. It was extremely difficult. But I can't just wait for Daesh to come and get us. I hope he understood this."

"Yes, I think he understands." Karin could hear Roza's shaky voice; she knew Roza would do anything for Yez and wanted to reassure her now. "He knows you are doing this to protect him, honor Ser and stop them from destroying Kobane. I agree," Karin said, touching Roza's arm.

"Thanks, Kar. I think he did."

"Have you met some of the women? They're very nice." Karin wanted to change the subject. Roza said she had met some of them. Karin could tell Roza needed a distraction and decided to take her to get some tea and food. She ushered Roza into the lounge room where they could drink black, sweet tea, and eat some flatbread and cheese.

***

After tea, the soldiers gathered in the sitting room. There was an old rusted heater on the side wall. Karin and Roza sat down on cushions next to Tanah and Torani. The Commander began to speak, looking each of the girls in the face as she continued;

"What is collectivism? I work for everyone, and everyone works for me. All for one and one for all. We're trying to build a life based on equality. We are not just thinking of the Kurds, but for all humankind, where we want to create a system our leader calls Democratic Confederalism. This is why we support democratic socialism. Ocalan's ideology spreads further than socialism and collectivism in Islamic societies. The mercy of Jesus Christ and Zarathustra's love of nature are combined in the Kurdish nation."

Karin's attention was sparked by the mention of Zoroaster and their ancient religion that her father and grandfather followed. This philosophy, Karin had read in Ocalan's literature, but now, in joining the YPJ, it was becoming so real. Going to the frontline, she may have to die to free Kobane from Daesh but also to fight against honor killings of women, child marriage, domestic violence and many other inequalities. She wanted to be part of this new future for women and men in this region. There was no other way.

"The YPJ is a movement to protect people's rights. The YPJ can give you strength, confidence, and the chance to fulfill your potential, girls. Here, we know we are someone, not a slave doing everything we are told by parents or a husband. But an individual someone, who has value and worth."

Just then a man came into the room, and motioned Commander Tolhedan over. There was Daesh activity nearby, and the men asked if she could help them. She excused herself from the group and told them to do their drill practice.

***

After the Commander returned, she set up targets for the women, and after loading their weapons, she got them to lie down and position themselves. Karin looked through the narrow iron sight and, lining up the tin can, shot one single bullet. The recoil pushed her arm and shoulder backward with a sudden and violent jolt. The first time she had shot her gun in the training camp was a shock, but now she was used to the feeling; the heaviness of the weapon and the pushback. Her arms and shoulders were developing substantial muscle and could take this impact.

She began to fire at the can, and hit it three times, causing it to fly from its position. Karin watched Roza; she had only just shot her first AK47 recently. Karin could tell she was still uncomfortable with it. But, even now after only a few days, she had seen Roza become more comfortable loading the weapon and firing at the practice targets. *After a few weeks of this, we will be ready. Though who knows if we will be?*

Karin gave a thumbs up signal to Roza, who smiled back. After some time practicing their shooting, the Commander said she was taking them to the frontline to show them how it would be, and to let them practice their skills. This was the only way to know what it would be like. They traveled by car. There were only five chosen from the battalion for the mission; Karin, Roza, Tanah, Torani, and Amara. They held their weapons to attention, facing the afternoon sky on the tray of the utility vehicle. When they arrived, Karin jumped out first, and the Commander followed.

"Go, Karin, check the inside of the house and then the roof. Torani you back her up. Roza, you check that building there, and Tanah, you check the walls for anything. Amara, you monitor the whole perimeter and look out for your comrades. In war, you'll have to protect each other."

Karin ran to the largely destroyed stone building. There was debris everywhere. She ran, crouching down, and looking around each doorway cautiously as she reached them. Her gun was always pointed forward, towards any possible threat, at a 45-degree angle. She checked the room and ran outside, and the Commander called, "Check the roof, Karin." Karin ran up the stairway on the side of the sand-colored building, crouching down slightly, in case there was enemy fire, or they were in sniper range. Pointing her gun into every crevice, she checked all the corners of the roof.

"All clear, Commander," she called. The others had completed their missions and were coming back to the group. The Commander signaled for them all to file back and leave. It was enough for today. They had not been shot at, but Karin felt it was a good introduction to what the adrenalin and fear may feel like on

84

the frontline. Filing into their group again, Karin felt there was now a strong bond between all of them, and a trust that they would defend each other in life and death.

"Good work, *haval,* let's go back." The Commander patted Karin on the shoulder. They jumped onto the back of the truck and rode back to the base as the sun was setting, in glorious pink and blue over the ancient quiet hills.

***

The following day Karin, Roza and the others went to visit Sercan's grave in Kobane. Karin would go and see Mani's grave as well when she was there. The soldiers had dug Mani a grave, with a few things that represented him on top of the soil, and a stone erected with his name drawn on it in black pen. Karin had not visited it yet, but she knew she had to also be there for Roza at Sercan's grave. Karin didn't like to show her emotions. She preferred not to show any at all. But if Roza needed to cry, she would be there for her. She decided she would ask to ring her parents when they got back. There was a special mobile phone designated for this.

Over these weeks in the training camp, Karin had begun to feel completely different. She was now more focused, in control of the weapons, her emotions, and able to devise strategy within minutes. The combination of physical training, weapon education, and the philosophy behind their movement was an ideal combination for Karin. It allowed her to see with the holistic view, and she could feel herself transforming from a civilian, studying medicine, to a soldier who would have to take life.

She still didn't like this prospect, but felt she had no choice—she would not let them come for anyone else she loved.

- 8 -

Roza

Commander Tolhedan had told them they could visit the hastily-created cemetery for the martyrs in Kobane. Roza was keen to visit Sercan's grave there and put some artificial flowers she found in the house on his grave. Also, she wanted to be near him again.

A few of them got onto the back of the Toyota Hilux and drove through YPG occupied territory to the makeshift cemetery. When they arrived, Roza felt shaky. Karin had come with her and walked next to her, with her arm around her back. The Commander knew she had lost her husband in recent fighting. Roza looked at the plaques made of paper and plastic that had been stuck to the stones.

She finally found his grave; his photo was attached to the stone. Sercan looked at Roza from the image; she felt like his eyes were examining her. Her chest felt tight. His eyes penetrated, talking to her in other-worldly whispers. Overwhelmed, she dropped to her knees and touching his photograph, wept. Karin stroked her back with tears in her eyes. The Commander walked over to them.

"Do not cry, Roza. When he died, you took up his weapons, and you're fighting for him." She knelt next to Roza in the dirt. Karin moved back.

"Tears are for the weak," Commander Tolhedan said. Inside, Roza felt enraged, but she did not say anything.

"We must continue our fight. Freedom requires a sacrifice of some kind. Don't let the others see you cry. Tears are for the weak."

Roza said nothing. She nodded, but desperately wanted the Commander to go away. Possibly the Commander was not as kind as Roza had first thought, or maybe she thought this would make Roza stronger. Either way, she felt angry about it. Roza gently nudged her arm away. The Commander rose and called all the girls to one part of the cemetery. She gathered them around herself. Roza followed, looking down the whole time to hide the tears that had been constantly falling since she entered through the gate.

"Why did we lose so many of our people, so young?"

No one answered the Commander's question.

"Ocalan, our leader said, 'The truth about the fallen is that we are alive and must keep up our fight for them and the revolution.'" This confused Roza. *What did this mean? Yes, I'm alive, but I don't want to be, not without him.* She felt sure she would see Sercan again. This platitude irritated her now, seemingly empty.

"So altogether, one, two, three, 'Martyrs do not die, martyrs do not die!'" They chanted and sang together, clapping.

Roza joined in, feeling numb. *I guess she means they live on in our memories, but they also live forever in paradise. I don't want him in paradise yet; he belongs with us. It's not right.*

The Commander was right about one thing. Roza had taken up a weapon after Sercan died, and she felt determined more than ever now. On the journey back to their training base, Roza didn't say anything, but some of the women began to sing quietly. Karin had her arm around Roza's shoulder. Roza knew Karin was grieving Mani and had visited his grave at the cemetery too, and she knew Karin understood. That was all she needed.

Roza did not eat dinner back at the camp; she just went into their room. She borrowed the phone that was designated for contact with their families. Listening to Yez's voice made her tears flow again, and she tried to conceal the emotion in her voice. He asked when she was coming back, she said in a while, and he told her about how he had been helping his Nana to get food. She yearned to hold him and tell him it would all be okay, but at this point, what could she say?

Hearing his voice was both soothing and torturous, as she knew she had to keep going to defeat Daesh. Otherwise, Yez was in mortal danger. She hadn't wanted to say goodbye and sang him a Kurdish lullaby, like she always used to do. Finally, she told him she loved him and said, 'see you soon.' After she hung up, exhaustion filled every limb, and she fell onto the mattress, falling asleep quickly, emotionally and physically depleted.

***

Commander Tolhedan's mother was coming to the training camp as things were quiet on the frontline at the moment. Roza thought this was a lovely idea, and wished they could all have this freedom with their families. Standing with the other ladies, Roza greeted the Commander's mother at the entrance to their compound. Tolhedan ushered them all in and said, "Better to talk inside the house than out here."

They all filed into the lounge room.

"See, I told you I had a lot of daughters," Tolhedan said, laughing.

"Yes, may God keep them all safe for you." Her mother looked around at the thirty women who were standing or sitting. Some of them were touching her on the shoulder. Roza felt they must be missing their mothers, especially the ones who had to leave their home without saying goodbye.

Roza thought of her mother, Naze and how they had parted. They had talked briefly before she talked to Yez. Naze seemed to understand and was supportive now, but still, Roza felt a heavy weight pressing down on her chest. She slipped out quietly, hoping to have a cigarette. It was too hard to think of these things. Making her way to the back of the room, she went out onto the veranda. Karin had noticed she was gone and followed her.

"Hard seeing the mother, hey?"

"Yep, and for you?" Roza asked Karin.

"Yes, me too. I think Mama understood in the end, but it's hard to think of her and Dad."

"Yes, and Yez." Roza's voice was faint. Karin sat next to her on the wall and put her arm around her.

"I'm worried about our families staying in Kobane, Kar. Did we do the right thing?"

"Yes, Rozi. What other choice did we have?" Karin shook her head. "It's like you've said before; neither of us wanted to sit there and wait to be killed, or worse. We *had* to defend our families. As far as I have heard through intelligence, they are all doing okay. There is no Daesh movement in that area, thank Allah."

"That is good news, isn't it? I think about them constantly, and hope Yez is not scared."

"I know, Roz. We are doing our best. He is proud of you. I am sure of that."

"Thanks, Kar. I'm becoming impatient to get to the frontline. I want things to get moving. I came to fight."

"Yes, well, it will only be a matter of days. I have requested we stay together, you and me. The Commander agreed it would be a good idea."

"I'm so glad. Thanks, Kar, I couldn't do this without you. Part of me is comforted by being here with this family, but I have left Yez, so I also want to get on with what I came for."

"I'm grateful you're here too, Roz. I know what you mean. I'm going to miss the girls and Commander. If only it could be like this all the time…but some of us will have to face injury or worse…"

"Yes, better not to think too much about that. War is a bloody mess, but we have to remember what we're fighting for, our futures."

Roza put her head on Karin's shoulder. She didn't want to verbalize her inner fears anymore. Suddenly, she felt exhausted.

***

After three weeks of training, Roza marveled at how the women were now lined up in flawless symmetry. The Commander called out— "At ease! Attention! Shoulder arms!"—and the women moved in magnificent precision, no mistakes, no turning in the wrong direction, like a shimmering, dancing bird on display. Roza also moved in rhythm with everyone; they all moved as one organism.

She was impressed with her comrades, and the way that Tolhedan had successfully changed these civilian women into soldiers, through kindness and humor. Roza felt this was a highly unconventional technique for an Army Commander. Still, nothing in this situation was like the past, with women fighting equally to men, even being Commanders over men in the YPJ.

All of the shooting practice, frontline scenarios, drills, the physical training with grenades and guns, and the mindset sessions; all of this had slowly begun to harden their sinews for war. Roza felt that Tolhedan had been perfect for facilitating their change. She understood them, where they were from, and what they had been through. Tolhedan had been through all of it, as well. She would miss Tolhedan, Torani, Tanah, and the other women. A few of them might be stationed with Karin and herself, but not all of them.

They continued to stand at attention in line.

"The Martyred Berivan Academy is at your disposal, Commander!" Comrade Amara called out, standing at attention to the Commander.

"At ease, ladies," Commander Tolhedan said.

They all parted their feet and relaxed their gait.

"Another YPJ training has been completed today. I have done my small part in the revolution by seeking to train you effectively. I'm sad to say goodbye to you all. You have all done well and listened intently to me. I can see such a difference in you." Roza saw tears in her eyes, but also a determination. Roza felt emotion rising inside, but she had learned to suppress her emotions more now. Well, it was not completely possible. After all, wasn't it human to have emotion?

"We will meet again in victories. It doesn't matter where we are—any one of us may be wounded, killed, or reposted—but the important thing is completing our mission. It's what our fallen comrades would expect of us. The whole world is playing political games with us. Despite this, we need to fight our enemy, Daesh. I do not want any of you to perish. I wish you luck and more luck and more luck. I have sought to teach you everything I know. I hope you all know I have experienced everything you will go through. Think of me when it gets tough, and know that I will be thinking of you always. You are like my daughters—daughters of our revolution. You are strong and courageous women who can defeat Daesh." Her gaze paused on each girl individually. Roza blinked away a tear. Soon, they would find out where they would

93

be posted. First, they had to recite their creed and swear their allegiance to the YPJ cause.

Roza stood next to Karin, Torani, Tanah, and Amara. In unison, they had to repeat what Tolhedan stated, standing in front of them. They all placed their hands on the green and yellow YPJ flag, with a photo of Ocalan in its center. There was an AK47 positioned in the middle of the flag, representing how they would fight for the cause. The women's voices repeated the following oath:

"Based on a paradigm of a democratic society, an ecological society, and freedom of ideas, irrespective of religion, language, ethnicity, group or party, I take into account the idea of self-defense, based on the regulations of the YPG and YPJ. On this basis, before Kurdistan's fallen heroes," Roza's voice cracked as she said this, "by the people of Kurdistan, and my brave comrades in arms, I swear! I swear! I swear!"

"Thank you, *haval*, comrades," Tolhedan said, saluting them.

Roza and Karin watched the next group of soldiers pledging themselves to this oath. Everything was moving forward. Roza dreaded another goodbye, but she wanted it to be over and done. Finally, they came to the part of the ceremony where they found out who would be with them.

"Comrades, we have divided you into different areas. A battle has sprung up in Serekaniyi again. So, I wish to send Amara and Chichek to this."

Roza felt disappointed that Amara would not be with them.

"The next group is: Karin, Roza, Tanah, Reynaz, and Torani. You are all going to the frontline battle in Eastern Kobane. This is a fierce battle, but I have confidence in your focus and resolve. I know you will be okay." After she had read the names, Roza felt relieved; she trusted all of those women and was glad she would be going with them. Roza's main comfort was Karin, she couldn't be here without her.

As other names were called out, Roza was thinking of how they would be leaving soon. After receiving their allocations, the women stood up. The girls began to chant and clap in unison; "Women, Life, Freedom! Women, Life, Freedom! Women, Life, Freedom!" Then they embraced. Roza clapped as well and joined in, if a little quieter than the others.

"Now, say your goodbyes. You need to get packed and leave straight away." Roza hugged Amara strongly, as did Karin. Comrade Chichek and others approached and hugged them. Roza felt sad, and slightly sick as well. This was now very real and scary. Was she ready? Was Karin? She walked over to the Commander. "Thank you so much for everything," she said. "We would not be able to do this without you."

"*Zor spa*s, Roza, it has been my pleasure to train you."

"Thank you for posting me with Karin."

"Of course. We can see the bond you have, so we didn't want to separate you. I wish you all the luck in the world," she said, embracing Roza in a hug. Karin also walked up and embraced Tolhedan. Roza was surprised by the fact that Karin didn't have any words; she seemed a bit overwhelmed. She didn't hear what was said as she moved away a little but could feel the emotion. Roza and Karin collected their bags from the room. There wasn't much to take to the front line, just warm clothes, and weapons. They didn't have many possessions. Roza touched the purple scarf on her neck and thought of Sercan and Yez as she jumped up on the back of the truck. She helped Karin up. They were as ready as they would ever be, at least Roza felt much more prepared now after the camp. She looked at Commander Tolhedan and smiled, forming the victory sign with her fingers, she hoped that one day they would be reunited. The Commander signaled back to Roza, smiling.

As the trucks began to move away, the women called out their mantra and clicked their tongues in their high-pitched, defiant declaration. The women's vehicles moved in different directions, away from the security of the training camp, and into their new existence where safety was a luxury. Roza leaned on Karin as they watched the buildings and surroundings pass. Driving towards the frontline, which was her home, Roza knew it would somehow be like a foreign place in many ways. She dreaded being there, especially now that Ser was gone. Roza's thoughts turned to Yez; she prayed as she breathed out that he was safe. She glanced over at Karin briefly and hoped they were both prepared for this. They were together, and that was all that mattered right now.

- 9 -

Karin
Late December, 2014
Kobane Frontline

Dawn colors of delicate pink mingled with dusty blue and rich orange as the sun rose over Kobane. Karin often found herself waking up with the sun on the frontline. It had been nearly four weeks since they left Commander Tolhedan. Karin and Roza had become acclimatized to the deathly chaos, confusion and bloodshed of the frontline. Sitting on the roof of the compound, she gazed at the sunrise. It seemed defiant to her, beauty persisting in the face of desolation.

She never slept more than five hours a night; images of death seemed to seep into her dreams. It was Karin's ritual, when combat didn't require her early, to sit and take in the breathtaking sunrise. In the corner of the veranda, she had set up a candle, broken and chipped, that she found in an abandoned house. When she came up here alone, she would light it in honor of Mani and Sercan, and the other martyrs they had lost. This was why she was here, after all. She found it peaceful and meditative to do this; it refocused her for the day. As Karin surveyed the devastation of Kobane, she longed to hear the call to Fajr prayer, ringing through the crisp air. Maia would perform the prayers in the front room, falling on her face onto the intricately decorative mat. Maia always wore her headscarf. Aster always rose early, but he could be found out in the olive groves tending to his land. Maybe this was his form of prayer. Dawn was sacred to Karin; it was her space where she could breathe and pause from the war. She needed it.

Now, Karin hoped her parents were okay in the Western part of Kobane. She would speak to them soon on the phone. There were reports from other soldiers and contacts that went over to that part of Kobane that their families were okay. But still, Karin thought of her family constantly, and Yez as well. She hoped they were able to eat well and were not too afraid. Now, she looked out on the ancient city of Kobane, where the soil used to yield rich pistachio trees, and her culture of song and dance was lived out in vitality and vibrancy. In its place now, were buildings obliterated by bombs, with whole sections of walls torn out, gaping chasms in the white structures. Day and night, red, orange, and yellow explosions lit up the sky and scorched parts of Kobane. The trees that used to provide shelter on the hills were annihilated and torn in half. The streets where she used to have coffee with Roza and Sozan or walk to the market for pomegranates and pistachios were now silent, save for the sounds of artillery, shelling, tanks, and trucks. Where Karin once avoided cars, buses, bikes, and mule carriages in the streets, there was emptiness and silence.

Sitting here, she prayed to the God of her ancestors for protection, resilience, and strength to fight another day. She gazed over the devastation touched by the sunrise now and lit up a cigarette; she always smoked at sunrise. It felt exhilarating and liberating. Karin felt the rush to her head and watched the smoke flow from her mouth. She reflected on Tolhedan's words about the society she wished to create after this hell. Pausing was her way of surviving, reflecting, otherwise she may be overwhelmed by the death all around them.

She closed her eyes and could see Aster, could smell his old deep blue coat, the scent a mixture of grass, tobacco, dirt, and the sweet aroma of olive oils. She longed to feel his arms around her and the softness of his white beard on her face. Maia's round middle and the purple and red scarf she wore most days came into Karin's mind. Maia had been opposed to her study in the beginning: "It wasn't what a woman should do." She remembered loud arguments with Maia before she left for Damascus University, and it had taken a long time for their relationship to repair. She missed her mother's throaty, loud laugh from the kitchen, and her bright tone of voice at the beginning of every day.

Sometimes at night, she saw images of the men she had killed in the past month of fighting, their glance of terror before she opened fire and they fell backward. She saw how young some of them were; she also saw Mani's gaze and was haunted by his eyes. Did he look like these Daesh men, when they beheaded him like an animal under the sun? Images of his terror and his last moments drove her. He must have been terrified with a mask over his face; she hoped that *Xwa* had been with him. Honestly, she felt confused about the God of her religion. The kaleidoscope of colors in the sky made her long for escape from this ugliness, but she knew there was no escape, not for her. She would not leave this battle until Kobane was free from Daesh. She stood up, blew out the candle in the corner, took one last look at the sunrise, stubbed out her cigarette, and went downstairs.

Later that morning, they had positioned themselves on the roof that looked into the building where Daesh was situated. Karin touched the leather band on her wrist, its soft, pliable qualities under her fingers. Mani had been dabbling with leatherwork. Touching the leather, she remembered when he had given it to her. He had walked up and fanned open his hand, saying, "Don't lose it. It's precious, you know." He had his characteristic smirk, and he winked, signaling irony. She had grabbed him into a sisterly embrace and said, "Yes, it is. I won't." How would she know at that time that a piece of leather would become so precious to her? It was also special that Aster had reminded her to wear it. She wore it always now, even though sometimes it got in the way as she positioned her AK47 in the dirt on the veranda where they were now. She poked the shaft of her gun through the purpose-made hole.

"Hey, you're too close, Kari," Roza said to Karin, pushing her sideways with a slight grin. Karin laughed and looked at her friend of more than 21 years.

"Okay, okay…hold your fire…" Karin said, holding her hands up in mock surrender. Sozan was positioned behind them, looking through another small hole in the wall.

"You two…" she said, rolling her eyes and shooting them a knowing look over her shoulder. They laughed. Karin had been relieved when they were stationed with Sozan, and thankful she was safe.

Karin and Roza readjusted their position. Karin felt as if she would swallow the dirt but had learned how to hold herself away correctly. They moved closer to the roughly cut holes in the small wall and looked through the tiny gap in the uneven concrete. Karin could only make out shadowy figures darting behind windows and walls in the building opposite them. Immediately, they began firing their machine guns through the holes.

She aimed at one of the Daesh men moving around in front of the window and aligned her iron sight on the end of the shaft with his figure. Focusing, she paused. Everything seemed to slow down and zoom in. She could only hear her breath; it was as if there was no one around her. Then she fired—shattering glass, and the man fell. Men began to move in more rapid motion now. More fire continued towards Karin and Roza. She didn't know if the man she had shot was dead or injured, but she continued to line up the men that appeared in the windows, picking them off one by one. They were only fifty meters from her.

Karin blinked away the dust in her eyes. Her rifle, though thin in size, was heavy with its combination of stamped steel and wood. Its trigger was rough, and its features were rudimentary compared to more modern weapons. Every time she released the magazine, its recoil felt like being shoved backward. Strangely, Karin was attached to her dirty, grimy old gun. She liked that it was tough and didn't need daily cleaning. Her gun endured sand and dirt but always remained reliable.

Karin shot directly into the second story window, where she knew there was a fighter. She saw white smoke and dust billowing from the building. Now the smoke obscured some parts from her view. Then she aimed at another section of the building and fired until she saw another figure fall. Three Daesh fighters abandoned their positions and began running to the left of the building. Disoriented it seemed, they ran in zig-zag formation, their black clothing making them look like figures in a silent Charlie Chaplin film Karin had seen many years before. They ran into the distance down the dusty white slopes. Karin stood up but quickly crouched again once she located them, and shot multiple times towards the closest one. The small figure fell face forward and no longer moved. The other man kept running and was fast retreating beyond their reach. Roza stood up and aimed at the figure that darted across the field. She began to shoot; the sound of high-pitched, metallic fire deadened Karin's ears, then silence. The first one fell, then the other one as well. All dead.

Karin patted Roza's arm. They both smiled and remained behind the wall, shrinking down beneath it. Daesh militia were still only a few hundred meters away; they could not rest for long. The battle for Kobane was crucial in this bloody war; they would not surrender. Apart from this being her home, Karin knew if Daesh gained this territory, they would occupy the whole region from the Euphrates River to the Turkish border. Kobane was a strategic corridor in which Daesh could transport weaponry between bases. She would not let this happen, not as long as she was alive. Karin, Roza, and Sozan went downstairs to their comrades, and restocked their weapons to resume their assault on the building.

***

That night Karin walked towards the blazing red and yellow fire, outside the compound up in the hills, behind the two disheveled buildings. Soldiers had to be on guard to watch for any unwanted visitors. The war never stopped, but occasionally they were able to pause. This part of Kobane had been won back from Daesh, and the city was divided into two sections. Hearing the soothing sounds of female voices singing in harmony, she approached the fireside, and saw some of her fellow soldiers eating. Roza was sitting on the small stone wall. Karin walked closer and sat down next to her, nodding hello to Sozan, Torani, Tanah, and Reynaz.

Karin had never thought Roza could become a soldier, but she was turning out to be much tougher than she had estimated. She had defended Karin many times, standing up and shooting assailants. Maybe what she suffered at the hands of her uncle enabled Roza to find this courage inside herself, or maybe she just didn't care about anything anymore. *Probably, both. Either way, Roza is fierce now.*

Looking at Roza's long black hair falling over her shoulders, Karin thought she still didn't look like a soldier. But then again, what did a soldier look like? They embraced hello, kissing each other on alternate sides of the cheeks, with a third kiss for emphasis. Karin leaned on Roza's shoulder slightly and sighed, though no one could hear it with the loud din of voices echoing around them. They needed these nights, warmed by the fire and each other. Roza gave her a small section of orange, and she took it and bit into it. It reminded her of the day she found out about Mani's death.

Karin raised her head, taking in the sweet melodic sounds of the gentle voices singing. She reveled in the sound of Jusef playing the *tembur,* his rhythmic strumming and the rich syllables of the language. Kar.in closed her eyes; she could see Ahman when he was given his new *tembur* for his tenth birthday. His eyes expanded and he didn't speak; he just stroked the smooth wood and began to strum, looking at Karin with a wide, joy-filled, white smile. His fingers explored the instrument, but also seemed to know it like it was part of his body. After this, he took lessons from a local man learning traditional Kurdish songs, and, at night, he would play for the family. Tears formed on the edges of Karin's eyes now, mingling with the dirt. She focused on Roza singing, her voice was strong and full. Her emotion wouldn't overwhelm her here, right now. All of the voices around her created an otherworldly effect, a beautiful parallel world to where they sat amidst this chaos. She decided to think about the possibilities of the society she was fighting for, where women and men were equal, and her people had greater autonomy in Syria.

- 10 -

Roza
Kobane- Frontline
December, 2014

R oza adjusted the purple scarf around her neck and combed her hair slowly as she looked into the cracked mirror. Quietly, and carefully, she walked in a meditative state to the makeshift cemetery to see him. This time, she was alone. *Thank Allah for that.* She felt completely numb, as if she couldn't feel her limbs, or the physicality of her legs moving one after the other. In the field, there were mounds of dirt above the graves of those they had lost. Then, Roza saw his grave and her yellow and red flowers from the last time she was here. Her thoughts turned to Yez and her parents; she prayed a prayer that they were still well. She felt sick thinking of Yez in danger.

"I'm sorry, Ser," she whispered, faintly. "I don't know what I'm doing. I don't know if I've failed you and Yez. I don't know if I'm doing the right thing. I hope you're proud of me. I wish you could talk to me. I need your wisdom. I didn't know what else to do. But I know one thing..." She fell onto her knees in the dirt, touching the stone they had placed on his grave. "I miss you so much. Sometimes I don't want to breathe..."

Roza buried her face in her hands and wept. She had been on the front line for a month, and three weeks with Tolhedan before this. Even though she had been here a short time, it felt like years. But she still remembered the first time she actually shot a Daesh man, as he ran down the street. She was positioned above in a window. When she released the gauge of the weapon, there was a strong push back, and she watched this man get hit with the bullets; he paused, seemingly in slow motion, then crumpled in the middle of the dirt road.

It was strange to see a connection between her fingers, some wood, metal, and powder, and taking a man's life. Instantly, she felt sick. An emptiness she had never experienced seemed to open up inside like a cavernous ravine, as she watched his deep thick blood oozing into the dirt. It hadn't gotten easier, but she was used to it, especially when Roza thought of how Ser's body and face, bloody and mutilated. When she saw men running toward her or their position, or they received enemy fire, she shot without thinking, pausing, or feeling anything. Commander Tolhedan would be proud of her.

Something inside had switched, from English teacher, mother, wife, to soldier. She felt nothing, except relief that it was not hers or her comrade's life that was lost. It had taken a little while, but she preferred how it was now. It meant she could get the job done. Being robotic was good. A robot was more likely to survive and to be able to protect others than someone who allowed themselves to feel. Feelings were not something she could allow to grow in this barren garden; they were dangerous. *Maybe*

Tolhedan was right. She didn't like to admit that. Roza walked slowly back to the base, looking around constantly with her machine gun poised at the front of her body. It felt as if she was a horse on a plain, with the flight instinct twitching under her velvety, soft skin. Roza walked into the discussion room and realized Commander Beritan was updating everyone on the next mission. Her cheeks warmed for a few moments in embarrassment, but she quickly sat down cross-legged at the back next to Sozan. She watched Commander Beritan tuck a pencil behind her ear. Roza had seen the Commander do this so many times; she would chew its edge when pondering or explaining the military strategies, targets, and positions of Daesh.

Commander Beritan had deep, dark circles under her eyes. She leaned on the wall to relieve her aching feet and legs as she stood in front of the female soldiers. A few were still coming in, but most sat in their uniforms cross-legged before her on the carpet, awaiting instruction. She had come from battle in Mount Sinjar, saving Yazidi refugees, and held a senior position in the army. Beritan had an air of authority about her, but Roza loved that she laughed with abandon. The Commander adjusted her green, squarish cap that restrained her thick, black curls, and turned towards the map to demonstrate what the mission would be.

"Today, we are moving our operations to Mishtenur Hill. Our YPG counterparts have intercepted Daesh coms, and know they are positioning themselves so they can retake Mishtenur. We know the hill is important; if they control this strategic position again, they will possess the radio tower. We all know this could give Daesh a strategic advantage over us. There are about fifty men who are advancing, and we can't let them take it. We will not surrender it." Commander Beritan paused and looked over at Roza and the other women.

"Now, we must move our operation slightly; intelligence has informed us they are housed in the courthouse buildings near the Hill. The YPG has set up some areas, and we will fight next to them." She began to identify areas on the map. Roza watched, but somehow could not focus. Her limbs were weary from the day before, and she slumped forward. Karin was sitting in front of her and seemed to be taking it all in. It reminded Roza of when they studied science in school, Karin always looked intrigued and enraptured.

"US air strikes are ongoing which will help us today. Even though we have battled on our own this far, it's excellent to have this help. The US is working with us, and we have been instructing them on the best targets to hit. They will be destroying the two key communication buildings we identified; this will allow us to continue to attack Daesh more aggressively. It will allow us to get closer to the buildings a few streets north of here and make even further progress into Daesh's bases. We will never give up. Let's go out again today and *Xwa* willing, we will be back tonight. I want us to be able to celebrate another victory."

The women called their collective cry in unison, the call that terrified Daesh men and threatened their hopes of heaven. They chanted loudly and in unison, as they always did, "Women, freedom, life!" and raised their weapons to the sky. Roza did as well, though with more weariness. The women began to stand up and move out to jump onto the back of the vehicles for the next mission.

Roza and Karin carried their AK47s and ammunition and pulled themselves up onto the back of a white utility vehicle, pointing their guns to the sky. They drove through the desolate streets and surveyed the damage of the buildings, holes in the walls, rubble where buildings had stood. There was nothing living. Trees had been flattened or torn apart, and Roza saw a sign for Mazar's Bakery, where she used to get bread. The sign was sliced into many pieces and the building was half flattened. It was a skeleton of the city Roza loved. It wasn't safe to drive through the streets— there were often snipers in the buildings. Roza scanned the doorways and windows as they passed. She did not speak to Karin, but the two sat close to each other and felt each other's body warmth. After fifteen minutes, they arrived at Mishtenur. The YPG, the male Kurdish forces, were already set up.

From the vantage point on the hill where the YPJ had started a new wave of attack, the sound of constant gunfire overwhelmed Roza's senses. In the distance, Roza saw red explosions and black dust and dirt ballooning into the sky. Fire appeared, igniting buildings in random succession. Powerful explosions from the YPJ forces moved forward, building by building. Roza could see Daesh fighters ducking in between buildings.

Roza and Karin lay behind a makeshift wall of sandbags and dug-out dirt, approximately 500 meters from the Daesh fighters. To her right, Yusef stood with a rocket-propelled grenade launcher, standing, aiming, waiting, until he pulled back, released and fired. The grenade launched with precision and sharp focus through the air, slamming into the building in front of them where constant fire produced waves of shrapnel all around them.

Down the hill from Roza, there were buildings in pieces, with walls blown off, floors in sections, and buildings reduced to rubble. She could see men and women from the YPJ and YPG hiding in crevices firing their automatic and semi-automatic weapons. They looked like small creatures hiding in burrows in the earth. Squares were blown out of buildings, and she could barely recognize the city where she grew up. Roza adjusted her gun and started to fire, keeping down low. Yusef and Agir laughed as their gunfire and the launcher impacted another building where Daesh lurked. She looked over at them and rolled her eyes. What were they doing? Typical Yusef. Roza could not believe the cavalier attitude he had; he often made jokes while buildings were falling around them. In a way, she welcomed it; it broke the traumatic din of war, but made her miss Sercan's humor, his teasing her about how he made tea better than she did.

The day continued in close combat with the twenty Daesh soldiers in the buildings below them. Fifteen Daesh men were killed, and now the YPJ could reclaim this street as they were doing all over Kobane. Walking back to base, Roza was flooded with loyalty and pride towards her fellow women soldiers. She couldn't believe she could feel this bonded with them. She had known Karin and Sozan all her life, but the others she had only met weeks ago. But she would willingly give her life for all of them. She put her arm around Karin and Sozan, and her thoughts turned towards Yez.

***

Later that night, Roza sat bolt upright up in her bed. Looking around as her eyes adjusted to the darkness, she saw the sleeping bodies in the room. She was breathless, and her chest felt tight

110

from her dream. Yez had been standing in the sunlight. His smile reflected a desert sunrise, pure and intangible as he called to her, "Mama!" His joyful abandon made her smile as he ran and embraced her. She felt his whole body against hers. She could smell the dirt in his thick, straight, black hair. She had called him Yezdanser because it meant 'Lion of God'—she had hoped he would embody this strength. His arms wrapped around her and his face perfectly fitted into the space between her head and neck, as if it was designed to be there. Then suddenly, she was in another place, and there was red everywhere, like cellophane wrapped around everything in the dank room.

She felt tightness in her chest; a claustrophobic, suffocating sensation seemed to be closing in on her. Roza saw Yez's large dark eyes and thick eyelashes saluting the sky. Around her body, she felt restricted, confined, like something was on top of her or holding her down. She could still see Yez's face, but now it was contorted in pain and agony. He was calling out to her, "Mama, Mama!" but she couldn't answer. She screamed, feeling fabric around her, and tried to call out to him, but the purple and red material began to close in on her face, and she screamed and screamed and could no longer see him…

Roza sat up straight in bed. Her breath was short and sharp as she adjusted her comprehension of reality. It felt as if someone had thrown cold water on her face. What did that dream mean? The bodies of her closest friends asleep around her did not provide the peace she hoped for. She felt fear in her quickened breath now, despite her rationality reassuring her. There was a void without Yez, and nothing could fill this.

Strangely, though the unbearable emptiness she had felt in the camp, like a gaping chasm with a howling wind, was in some ways, alleviated by battle. Fighting Daesh, pushing them back, protecting her friends and herself; seeing Daesh men run away, she had to admit, didn't fill the chasm, but it replaced how she felt with purpose. Every morning she would wake up to a new mission, transported to a new position and to fight, yes, to kill, to free her people. She would never have thought she could kill anyone, but when machine guns were firing, and the thin men in black were running towards her everything changed. It became focused down to split seconds for Roza, and decisions made in those moments. When a man with a black beard is yelling "Allah Akbar" in a hysterical tone and is running towards you or if someone is shooting from a position on a building, everything slows down, and life becomes very clear. Kill or be killed.

In those moments, she felt something other than devastation about Ser. It was living on the edge of life and death that had made her feel *something* again; had made her feel, ironically, alive. She was fighting for Sercan, Yez, and the future of women in Kobane. Daesh would not take their freedom. They had taken nearly everything from her now, but they would not win.

Roza looked at Karin lying asleep, and Sozan snoring next to her. No one else in the room stirred. Roza's grief felt intensified by the darkness of the room; she needed to get out onto the veranda. She got up, took her cigarettes from under her pillow, and picked her way carefully across the floor so as not to disturb the bodies in slumber. Sleep was a precious commodity here. She hoped Yez was safe where they were. Thinking about him now, she could barely breathe. In that part of Kobane, there were people

112

all staying together in a few houses. They were all banding together, sharing food and protecting each other. This was why she was here, to stop Daesh getting over to that part of the town. She hoped that he understood she was fighting for him—for his Dad, her parents, everyone. Walking outside into the cool night air, Roza inhaled deeply and slowed her breathing. The silence soothed her. A mass of blackness, packed with glittering perfection, crowded the canopy above her. A star streamed across the sky as she looked, dying as it went. There was a white wall around their compound that protected them from the enemy. Everything was silent, except for the rhythmical, reassuring sound of crickets clicking. Roza lit up a cigarette, inhaling the smoke and blowing out a stream of air into the night. She had only started smoking since the war. Of course, women were not permitted to smoke, but Roza had long passed the boundaries of what women should or shouldn't do. Should a woman have to leave her only son to protect him and push back the enemy? Smoking made her feel liberated.

There was a distant sound of voices, probably the men from the YPG next door to them. Roza was grateful for them; they worked well with the female forces and would often follow the orders and direction of the YPJ's lead soldiers and Commander. Of course, there were a few men who were skeptical about women soldiers, but they had seen women fighting successfully for Kurdish liberation within the forces for a long time now. Women soldiers were not foreign to the men, and were seen as indispensable.

There would only be a few men up on guard in case the enemy attacked at night. The YPG male battalion was outnumbered by women in this battle; Roza thought this was interesting since the battle of Kobane was seen as the roughest fight yet in the war against Daesh. The stillness almost made her forget what the days held; the shellfire, the constant sound of machine guns, the explosions, and the cheers when they blew up the enemy or a house that they used. Sometimes she had a high-pitched ringing in her ears, the cacophony of war, the sounds assaulted you as much as anything else. There was a noise behind her; something was there. Someone touched her back. She jumped and swung around to see who it was.

"What are you doing up?" Karin said, putting her arm around her friend.

"Couldn't sleep."

"Nightmares, again?"

"Yes, with Yez."

Karin put her arm over Roza's shoulder. Roza offered Karin a drag. She took it and inhaled.

"I hope Yez is okay." Roza looked out into the darkness.

"He is. He knows you're fighting for him."

"Sometimes, I just think: what life will he have if he loses me?"

"If it happened, God forbid, he has your family, who would look after him. I will do everything I can to prevent that, Rozi."

"I know. Thanks, Kari," she said, turning to face Karin.

"You don't have to stay, though. You have fought so well in this battle. Ser would be proud of you. But you don't have to stay."

"I can't stop now, Kar." Roza didn't want to say that being in battle made her feel close to Sercan again, that she was continuing what he started, and somehow, she felt connected to him here.

"Yes, me either," Karin said.

"God willing, we'll be okay."

"Yes, *Xwa* willing," Karin said, with dullness in her tone, as she turned outward to the darkness.

Roza knew Karin loved Yez like a son. She would play soccer with him in the alley, and she remembered how she would ruffle his hair and hug him after a goal. Yez would put his arm around Karin's middle and walk back to the house with her for a drink. She remembered one day seeing Yez running after the ball and tripping over onto his face. For a moment, nothing could be heard until he caught his breath, and Karin ran to his side; then his screams started. She picked him up in her arms, and he buried his head into her, his leg bleeding, and his face cut.

"Let's get you a bandage," Karin had said, as she placed him carefully on the ground near Roza.

"Does your head feel okay?"

"Yes," he had answered, and Karin had gone inside the house to get her bandages.

Roza took another drag of her cigarette, and thought about how Karin had almost married Terah and had children of her own, but didn't want to have to abandon her desire to be a doctor. Occasionally, Roza had seen a glimpse of melancholy cross Karin's face when she looked at Yez. Then again, Karin reveled in her freedom to fight, to be part of this greater cause of the liberation of women, and for that she needed to have no constraints except her obligations to her parents. Roza couldn't help but think that Karin had no idea how it felt to be separated from her only child.

"We should get some sleep," Karin said.

"Yes, we should. I'll be there soon."

"Don't worry Roz, as much as I can I'll protect you and remember, they're not as terrifying as they make out." Karin winked at Roza with a wry grin. Roza smiled as well. She had seen Daesh men run in fear from herself and her female comrades, petrified they would lose their 72 virgins and heaven if killed by a woman. She had seen cowardice first-hand in the eyes of the men she had killed. She was confident victory would be achieved soon, though occasionally doubts surfaced.

"Very true," Roza said, laughing. "They are cowards before us."

"Yes." Karin also laughed, touched Roza's arm, and went back inside.

Roza wanted to stay out here all night in the stillness; she knew the sun was coming and with it all the noise, chaos, and death. She closed her eyes and pictured Yez running towards her when she returned home. She felt his arms around her neck as he jumped into her embrace. His face was close to hers, where it was meant to be.

- 11 -

Karin
Frontline Kobane
December 15, 2014

A fter eating some flatbread and drinking black tea, Karin and Roza carried their rifles and ammunition up the stairs to the roof, walking in silence. There was already gunfire coming from the building across from them. Daesh had been moving progressively towards the YPJ and YPG forces, and had taken the opposite building the day before with an estimated forty men inside. They had occupied fifty percent of the city, and Karin was proud that Daesh had now been pushed back to thirty percent. Eventually, they would be forced out of Kobane.

This position on the hill was a key vantage point, and the Commander had emphasized to Karin how important it was for them to be ruthless and unyielding. To Karin, courage always seemed to be attributed to men and yet, in her experience in this war, it had been shown to have no gender. Often Karin and her comrades would watch the Daesh propaganda videos; they didn't watch the killings though. This Karin could not watch. But Karin and Roza would watch them and find them amusing, as when they encountered Daesh, some of them were teenagers, and scared men, running down the streets and laneways, fearful of being killed by women. They were not ferocious or tough. Often drugs were found on their bodies, and Karin felt this was another sign of weakness; they needed to be high to do what they were doing. It was also a contradiction to the religion they were supposedly fighting for, as well. Daesh men scuttled away from the armed women, desperate not to lose their 72 heavenly virgins. Karin's battalion used the high-pitched battle cry that instilled fear into Daesh, calling it just before launching a surprise attack. This war was challenging many things, allowing women to come out of being confined to only one path. Karin embraced the chance to fight for this freedom, even if she died to achieve this for others.

Karin pushed back her thick, black hair, soft on its ends. She often wanted to cut it all off like a man. She fought like a man, wore a uniform, felt the burden of a machine gun, and wore bullets geometrically lined up over her shoulders. She trained for combat like a man, killed like a man and watched people die in the dust—why should she not also have a short haircut? It made no sense to her. But she did not cut it out of respect for her mother, for whom a woman's hair was her "glory." Instead, every morning Karin pulled her hair back into a tight and rudimentary bun.

The building they lived in was made of concrete blocks, with paint-peeling walls and an open fire stove. Their beds were a blanket and cushion on the floor. There was a cracked mirror on the wall in which to check their appearance. Karin never saw the point of worrying about her hair, unless it was in the way. Once Karin and Roza reached the rooftop, they got into position to

119

begin an assault. Hours later, Karin rubbed her eyes. Her armpits ached, and her rib cage was sore from kneeling and lying down facing the hole in the wall for hours in combat. She was allowed a break, and she went downstairs. From the lounge room, Karin saw Sozan sitting in the courtyard of the compound with her legs crossed and an AK 47 on her lap. Smoke formed big masses around Sozan in the still, dense air. She was slight in build, but had a spirited look about her, like a white Arabian horse; flighty, fierce, fast, and beautiful. In civilian life, Sozan always spoke her mind, but in battle, Karin had seen her become more withdrawn and troubled, though Karin still saw the old Sozan in the yellow reflected from the center of her green eyes.

Sozan's blonde hair, dyed months ago, had now begun to show dark roots growing from the scalp. Blonde hair had made Sozan stand out, but then, she reveled in being different. Most women in this region, including Karin, had dark hair, dark eyes, and dark skin. Sozan had lighter colored hair and green eyes. Deep down, Karin knew Sozan had always felt different from everyone. Karin didn't know whether it was because her father would tell her she should change, 'be like everyone else,' just before he would beat her or throw her against the wall, or whether it was because she became a practicing Christian when she left home at sixteen. She always stood out, and liked it this way. Karin had always thought Sozan walked around Kobane as if she was already free, with humor and desire for something greater than herself.

Karin and Sozan always had conversations about how she wanted to travel the world, and see the beauty that existed, even though her family would never leave Kobane. She had even left her aunt and uncle without saying goodbye to join the YPJ; no one could stop Sozan doing what she thought she should. That was what Karin loved about her.

"*Silav*," Karin said, sitting next to Sozan on the wall.

"*Silav*, how are you this morning, sis?"

"I'm okay. My ears are ringing, though." She took out her small stash of cigarettes from her pocket. Now, Sozan's sister, Ashti, was in the hands of Daesh and freeing her was all Sozan thought about.

"How are you going, really?" Karin asked, touching Sozan's arm.

"Not good, Kar. I'm out of my mind with worry, for Ashti."

Karin was talking to Sozan about the need to talk to the Commander about tonight's mission and about finding Ashti, when out of the corner of her eye, Karin saw Elend approach.

"Hello, *haval*, comrade," she said, smiling at him.

"Hello. Are you well today?"

"I'm pretty good." Taking her small stash of cigarettes from her pocket, Karin noticed Elend looking at her with a smirk; he knew the rules for women. When their eyes met, she also saw in his gaze a certain tenderness and respect. They had fought side by side many times now in the past month.

"How are you?" Karin asked.

"Tekan died yesterday."

Elend looked down at his hands.

"I heard. I'm so sorry. Peace be upon him. What happened, Elend?"

"We were driving to the Kobane hill when suddenly we were fired at from all around us. There must have been a sniper above us. Tekan was talking to me about his brother over the border, and the next moment there was gunfire, and he was hit. Then he was gone. I fired back out my window, but his face was still. He was hit straight in the head." Elend looked down at the weapon on his lap and touched its dark metal. Karin went to touch his arm to comfort him, but pulled back, not knowing if he would be comfortable with this.

"I'm so sorry, Elend. He was like a brother to you."

"Yes…" He looked down again as if he wished he could hide in the folds of his clothes. Karin noticed Amez and two other soldiers walking close with a man who was bound up. She wondered what they were doing. Amez called out to Karin and Elend.

"*Silav*, Comrades."

"*Silav*," Karin said.

Karin noticed the man was dressed in black; could he be a Daesh fighter? For a moment, Karin's pulse quickened. She pulled her gun to the front of her body.

"It's okay, Karin," Amez said, seeing her alarm, "we have him under control. Have you heard about this man? His name is Mado. And we captured him on the Turkish border, fighting for Daesh."

Karin nodded, looking at the man suspiciously, and wondering where Amez was taking him.

"Well, we have had him for the last week, trying to feed him and clothe him and show we are good Muslim people like him."

"Really?" Karin looked again at the man. She thought he must have been early twenties; he had a patchy, thin dark, brown beard, and long dark eyelashes. His nose was pointy, and his body was wiry. His hands were bound in front of him, and his head was bowed down, looking at the ground.

"Yes, we wanted to see why he was fighting us. We even took him to the mosque to show him we are devout Muslims."

"Did it work?"

"Not really. You can ask him why; he will tell you."

"Okay," Karin moved toward the man who looked up, and she saw in his face a familiar alarm at her approach. "So…You look just like us, and you grew up around here, you know we are Muslims, most of us, why do you want to kill us?"
The man looked directly into Karin's face, and this time, his eyes were strong, determined, and unfaltering.

"Because Muslims are *Kaffir* too, infidels," he said.

Karin wanted to hit him in the face with her weapon but restrained herself. She inhaled her cigarette and blew it into his face, defiantly. He coughed and looked down again.

Karin pulled Amez away from this man to talk to him. Elend also joined them.

"He infuriates me."

"Yes, well, you know what they believe is coming—and he has told us to kill him, so he can go to heaven and receive his 72 virginal brides with his fellow soldiers."

"What?" Karin was becoming even more incensed at this man.

"Yeah, he said if we didn't kill him, he would blow himself up or somehow find a way to commit suicide and kill us as well."

"Oh, I see. So, what will you do? You can't really do what he wants, as it's against our policies," Karin said, gazing over at Mado. "It wouldn't be right."

"Yes, we don't kill our prisoners. Then we become like them."

"Even though I've killed Daesh in battle, I couldn't do it like this; it's not right," Karin said, thinking it felt strange to talk about the death of a man in such a clinical way, as if it concerned who would be washing the dishes after dinner. *The absurdity of this war gets worse every day.*

"I agree," Sozan said, looking at the Daesh man for a long time. His head was bowed, as he kneeled in the sand. He looked up briefly, his eyes darted between the four of them like a goat cornered by a mountain lion. Karin also looked at him. He must be terrified I will rob him of his one desire, she thought. She had seen this in many Daesh men she killed in combat before this, but today, being so close in proximity to him, this felt different.

"I don't envy your position," Karin said to Amez.

"Me, either. I think we will keep him like all the other Daesh men we have captured."

"Yeah, we don't want to be like Daesh. That's why we take our YPJ oath, and one of those principles is we don't do that." Karin touched him on the shoulder, going against conventions.

"Thanks, Karin, may *Xwa* be with you."

"And with you," Karin answered.

"Go well, please sis, remember Ashti" Sozan said.

Above them, the morning sky was vivid and perfectly blue. Beyond the compound, the sounds of war, constant gunfire, bombing, and explosions seemed to be a terrifying symphony, somewhat in the distance. But here, it was almost serene. White wag-tailed birds chimed above them. Karin glanced at the birds and wondered at how oblivious nature could be while the world around it crumbled. She watched the bird fossicking in the olive tree and remembered looking for nests of white wagtails with Mani. Amez nodded and walked over to the men holding Mado. Karin saw Mado was looking up every now and then from where he was kneeling not far away. He seemed to be trying to overhear what they were saying.

"Okay," Amez said. He signaled to the men they were leaving, and they pulled him up. As they did, Mado looked back into Karin's eyes with some kind of acknowledgment. Though she couldn't say exactly; it seemed like a flicker of relief, possibly gratitude from one human to another. Karin turned and walked a little way away. Sozan followed her. There were many things she had not fully understood about Sozan growing up, mostly her Christian faith, which others had teased her about when she converted. But Karin felt unified with her in war and loved her like a sister, always defending her and being protective of her. Sozan put her arm around Karin's shoulder.

"I hate this bloody war," Karin said. "It makes no sense, not that war ever does, I guess." She stubbed her cigarette in the dirt.

"Me too."

"We need to go now."

"Yes, we will go tonight. But we need to talk to Commander Beritan about it."

"Are you doing a night raid?" Elend asked.

"Yes, we are, due to intelligence from the YPG about soldiers that are in a building close to here."

"Well, may *Xwa* go with you and keep you safe," Elend said, standing up.

"Thank you very much, and you as well, Elend. See you soon," Karin said.

"Goodbye," he said. Karin looked at him, knowing there were never any guarantees in this life now. Karin and Sozan began to walk towards the building where Commander Beritan was discussing strategies with the other soldiers. The sun felt hot on their backs, and the dry air made Karin clear her parched throat. Even though at night it was getting cold, the days had hot sun, but cool winds at this time of year. Karin noticed Sozan seemed troubled.

"How are you going, sis?"

"I'm okay, Kar. I can't stop thinking about Ashti, ever since her capture. I have nightmares. We have to get her back, Kar." Sozan's voice was shaky. "It's been days since Amez told us about her capture with the other women. I feel like we're wasting time."

"I know, and we will act straight away. We need to make plans with the Commander. Ashti will be freed, definitely."

Karin knew that Sozan had been traumatized, as they all were when they found their friend Torah raped and dumped in the dirt outside Kobane.

"I can't even think about what she's going through," Sozan turned away and looked beyond the wall. "We have to get them back, no matter what. Can we talk to the Commander again? We need to act. I'm getting impatient."

"Yes, definitely. We will."

They walked into the building. Karin put her arm around Sozan and pulled her close. She remembered as young teens they would fly kites through the streets, even though it was only meant to be boys who did this. Karin and Sozan had never cared about such a stupid rule. How they had laughed and run, adrenalin pulsing through them as they felt the harsh gaze of people around them. They didn't care then, and wouldn't start now.

"I promise you, Soz, we will get her back. *Xwa* willing." Karin spoke with strength and conviction, even though inside, she felt doubt and fear.

"Thank you." Tears formed in Sozan's eyes. "I can't bear it." Sozan touched the silver cross that hung around her neck, traced its edges, and kissed it.

***

The night felt cool around Karin as she led Roza, Sozan, and Tanah through the still streets. Quietly, they crept like cats. They often had to venture out for night raids. Tonight, Karin was the leader; they crouched down and ran close to the buildings. Slowing down, they walked down the alleyway, being even quieter, the sound of muffled voices discernible as they edged closer to the target. There was a window they had seen next to the door. Moving closer to the door, Karin crouched and nodded to Roza to stay behind. She signaled to Sozan to move forward. Sozan, crouching low, moved just below the window then stood up, smashing her AK47 through the glass and shooting as she went. Karin then followed, the sound of sheering metal, screams, and gunfire piercing her ears. Karin released the grenade and threw it in. They only had one moment before it blew, and they all sprinted away as the building was torn apart, pieces of stone, shrapnel, and glass came flying after them. Screams filled the air of the men who were inside, injured, and possibly dying.

They ran. Karin felt her legs moving in robotic motion until her lungs felt as if they could explode. The rhythmic sound of their pounding boots in unison echoed through the desolate streets at 1am. Finally, they reached the street where their compound was. It was only then Karin realized that Tanah had been hit in the arm with shards of brick and rock and was bleeding profusely.

"How bad is it? Are you okay?"

"I'm okay," Tanah said, holding her arm. Karin tore her shirt and wrapped a bandage around Tanah's arm. Tanah moaned as her wound began to pulsate under the fabric.

"Anyone else hurt?" Karin asked.

They all had cuts on their faces and small holes in the fabric of their shirts. Shards of glass had sliced their soft skin into short vertical and horizontal lines like the top of a pie. Karin went over to Tanah. "Good work, Comrade." She supported Tanah and ushered her in to the support of other soldiers.

"You'll be okay. We killed several of them tonight, we believe. You did well."

Tanah managed a tentative smile and walked away with one of the women who carried a medical kit. They sat in the corner, and Sorah attended to her wounds.

Karin turned to Roza. "*Chawa ye?*"

"I'm okay."

Her face had a graze across its symmetrical elegance, just below her cheek line, and blood oozed down her face. Karin touched her face.

"Do you want me to attend to that?"

"I'll get Sorah to look at it," Roza said.

Karin went over to Sorah and asked if she could see to Roza's wound.

"What about you, Kar?"

"I'm fine, but you can check me after Roza."

Roza stood compliantly with Sorah and allowed her to check her body. Karin walked out to the veranda. Now, as she closed her eyes, she heard the men's screams again, felt the force of the explosion, white dust surrounding her and the deafening sound of shattering glass. It was always like this. Every day, the fighting played over in her mind like a film that would not cease. It was as if she was watching herself on film, like the Westerns they only occasionally saw in Kobane. The cinema screened romances, children's movies, and Westerns, but never with women playing the action heroines.

She lit up a cigarette and stood out under the olive tree in the compound. Closing her eyes, Karin inhaled the scent of the tree and was back in her childhood. Exhaling a column of grey smoke, she quietly thanked God for helping them to be successful in their mission tonight. Looking at the olive tree above her, the distinct smell of the branches and seeds took her back to their farm. Standing there, she remembered perching herself on her father's expansive lap under one of their olive trees, eating sweet oranges and letting juice run down her chin on Sunday afternoons.

Aster would sit below this tree while she and Mani climbed. He would let her climb as high as she could while watching with a satisfied smile. He laughed when she would call out to him to boast how far she had gone. She could see him smoking his pipe, packed with sweet-smelling, moist tobacco, and felt his calming, strong presence. Suddenly she felt an overwhelming weariness in her limbs. Karin hoped Aster was safe where they were and not worrying too much about her. Soon, she and Roza would ring their families again. She realized on both of her arms were many abrasions. She had to get disinfectant; the last thing Karin wanted was an infection. She touched Roza on the back as she walked past and smiled.

"Good work, Rozi."
"You too, Kar."

After they were all bandaged and had debriefed the Commander about the mission, she praised them for their success and told them to get some 'well-earned rest.' Mado came into Karin's mind; his face, his expression, the darkness of his gaze and the bags under his eyes. His uncertainty, combined with arrogance, haunted her. How could someone like him, who looked like them and was raised in their region, be so brainwashed to want to kill them at any cost? Her mind wanted an escape from this reality, like a horse wanting freedom from a wooden fenced enclosure. She needed relief. There was nothing Karin wanted more than to sleep. She fell onto her mattress, and tonight, sleep came quickly and mercifully, and blackness blanketed her in comfort.

- 12 -

Roza

Roza was pleased that today they would have a break from combat. Roza, Karin, and Sozan were visiting their journalist comrades in western Kobane, to see what they could find out about Ashti and the girls. It was better to do this in person, in case Daesh managed to intercept their conversations. Usually, the journalists came to the frontline to gather information about casualties and to report on what was happening.

Roza regarded these journalists as good friends now, since she had met them when they first arrived and had regular contact since. There was something about being around people who were present at the frontline, but in some ways on the outside of it. Being around them was a momentary respite for Roza, an escape from the trauma she and her comrades faced daily. The journalists understood how they felt; they also lived with the dangers of war on their doorstep, and had to be extremely careful. The three girls made their way stealthily through the holes in the houses to keep themselves hidden, keeping a watch out for anything suspicious.

"Kari, you can update Farhan?" Roza said, winking at her.

"Yes, you do that; we can update the others," Sozan said, a smirk crossing her thin lips as well.

"Come on, girls." Karin laughed at them, but Roza could tell she was a little embarrassed. *Kari deserves to have someone.* Walking behind Karin, Roza recalled how Terah, Karin's fiancée, had asked her not to continue studying to become a doctor and to follow him with his military career. When he asked that of Karin, Roza knew he wasn't right for her.

She had refused and tried to negotiate with him, but he couldn't understand. When their relationship broke up, Karin was devastated; she threw herself into her studies even more, and didn't socialize for months. Farhan, however, was a journalist from Kobane, who had studied journalism at Damascus University. He was intelligent, sensitive, and shared the same social values as Karin and Roza, for democratic socialism and equal rights. He was much better suited to Karin, Roza had felt, when they met him some weeks back. He had a dark sense of humor which suited Karin, and his features were dark and well-defined; he had high cheekbones and a thick black beard. His eyebrows were substantial and moved around as if they were only dancing on the top of his skin as he asked the girls questions. He had the longest and most elegant pianist fingers Roza had ever seen.

"There's nothing between us," Karin insisted as they continued to move through the walls.

"Sure, I believe you," Roza said, smiling at Sozan. After walking twenty minutes, they arrived at an unassuming cream building, previously it had been a house, now it was a newsroom of sorts. Here, male and female journalists interacted in a unique way, and Roza loved to see this. Out the front, an old man was sitting on a crate; he had white hair and a whiskery beard on his weathered, warm, face. He was rolling a cigarette with a white paper. Roza noticed his AK47 slung over his front. He reminded her of her grandfather.

"God be with you, Miss," he said.

"And you." Roza smiled and nodded to him. She felt like saluting him as a soldier, as she knew he had stayed to fight to the end. A little further off, Roza saw three men sitting against the wall. One of them was singing in Kurdish; *"Kobane is sad today, it's being destroyed, blood and corpses everywhere. Our eyes are shedding tears like rain."* She couldn't help but think the melody was beautiful and his voice soothing, even if it spoke of their pain.

As Roza moved towards the door, shelling shook the buildings nearby. Roza and the others moved inside. They were used to this and did not flinch with the sound. The building began to rattle with the bombing of the surrounding buildings. They entered the dark house as the mortar fire impacted a building close by. Even though this was not considered the frontline as they were in Western Kobane, Daesh was now attacking from nearly every side. Roza did respect immensely that these journalists had stayed surrounded by danger to report about Kobane from the inside out. The fact that they were not soldiers made it more admirable.

From inside, another resident white shepherd dog walked out of a door. Roza noticed his sores and patchy fur; he walked slowly and deliberately as if all of his limbs ached. They went down the side entrance, and Karin knocked on the door. A man opened it and smiled when he saw the three girls.

"*Silav*, Kari, Roza, and Sozan. Good to see you well," Farhan greeted them.

"Good to see you, too," Karin said, looking surprisingly nervous.

Roza nudged her. Three journalists were sitting on the couch. One had a laptop, connecting to Skype for an interview while they had internet, and another was talking on his phone. The building they operated in was powered by a loud generator outside. Another open-faced woman looked up at them from behind a laptop; she was trying to upload recent footage of the battles to YouTube. Roza recognized her as Nasrin.

"*Girls*!" She called out in a loud, ecstatic voice. "Good to see you!" Sozan went to Nasrin and kissed her three times.

"Great to see you, too."

Nasrin came and kissed Roza and Karin also.

"Come in, we'll have some tea. We need to talk about Ashti, and the girls, and the new tip-off we have: hopefully, this will be it. Also, you can update us as well."

Nasrin took them into the kitchen where she had a mat on the floor, and there was a woodfire stove. Filling up the kettle with water from a bottle, she put it onto the black metal plate. Farhan also came into the kitchen. He was wearing his AK 47 and had a belt of ammunition over his shoulder, as they had to stand watch at all hours. He sat down with them, taking off his weapon to be more comfortable. Roza looked at Karin. Karin was focused on Nasrin and seemed to be trying not to look at Farhan. However, he was looking at Karin, he couldn't help it. Roza found it amusing. Watching them both made Roza ache for Sercan; he used to look at her this way. *One of us should have this.* It helped Roza to see this attraction between them. It reminded her of the normal life that had long disappeared.

Roza began to tell Farhan that they had recently lost five people in heavy fighting, but had also killed more than fifteen Daesh fighters by blowing up vehicles and in hand-to-hand combat. They looked at the map the journalists spread out on the floor. Sozan pointed out their current positions and where the battles were ongoing; Karin chimed in with additional details.

"How's your reporting going?" Roza asked Farhan.

"Very good, thank you. We appreciate how you help us get the news out." He smiled at Roza. "I have, however, stopped interviewing fighters now."

"Why?" Roza asked.

"Because after I interviewed this brave young man at the beginning of the battle, I edited the footage and uploaded it to YouTube. Two days later, I was informed of his death in combat from mortar fire. After that, I decided not to interview people anymore. Too many people I have interviewed have died." He looked down at his camera.

"I understand, completely," Roza said gently. Sozan was sitting next to Roza, and after a few moments, she said, "Is it okay, if we talk more about Ashti and the girls, and where you think they may be?"

"Yes, of course." Farhan nodded to Nasrin. "We have received information that could lead us to your sister, Sozan. Hopefully, it will."

"I would be so grateful," Sozan said.

Roza saw Karin glancing toward Farhan, and noticed he was looking at her. Everyone leaned in closer as Nasrin explained the new information that a soldier had gained about a building they believed the girls were in. She pointed to the possible buildings on the map. The captured girls had contacted Amir on their mobile phone that one of them had managed to conceal. Amir called the journalists and passed on the details who contacted Sozan. But now it had become much harder now to continue contacting the forces.

Roza felt anxious about Ashti and the other girls, and prayed they would find them before they were shipped off like animals to more abusive men, disappearing out of reach. Sitting here now, listening to the information, reminded her of why she was fighting.

- 13 -

Karin

Karin didn't know why Roza kept bringing up Farhan; there was nothing between them. But Sozan and Roza had insisted they go to see the journalists. *It's important, I suppose*, Karin conceded. She admired how the journalists would sit up on watch just like soldiers, and how Farhan and Nasrin wore weapons to defend their press center, which consisted of a converted house in the west of the city.

After making their way to the house, which wasn't that far from the frontline, Karin knocked on the front door. It didn't look like a media headquarters, that reported vital news to the rest of the world. It was simply a house. Karin saw an old man sitting on the pavement who looked a bit like Aster, and he wished them well. She wished she could sit down with the old man and talk to him, spend time with him. Three men were singing in the corner of the building; the melody was soothing, as Karin felt strangely nervous. When she saw Farhan her stomach churned. She hated it, it was inconvenient. She just wanted to be normal and get the job done. She had sought to suppress all of these things in civilian life, but even more now. *Why should I get nervous when I don't have feelings for him?* But every time she saw him, it was always the same. She had always thought she was more rational than most women, not thinking about romance or seeking a partner, and yet she could not control her stomach and the rush of her adrenalin. Maybe it was because he always looked at her so intently, with his reserved manner. He would talk directly to her, and not stop looking with his intense, dark eyes, and wide smile beneath his beard. It was no different today. He smiled and welcomed them in.

"*Silav*, Kari, Roza, and Sozan. Welcome, come in. It's so good to see you well." He seemed genuinely relieved they were okay. They followed him in; other journalists and civilians were moving around in the house, discussing where they had to go next for information. As with most buildings within Kobane, Karin heard the whirring of the generator that produced electricity for the journalists. She knew the journalists accessed Wi-Fi internet from across the border in Turkey, and smiled wryly, thinking of how ironic it was in this battle. A girl sat on the ground with a laptop. It was Nasrin, and she greeted them loudly. Karin noticed the disheveled white dog she had seen here before. She patted his old frame as he walked past her, and he turned and licked her on the hand, then walked slowly outside.

"Girls! Good to see you!" Nasrin ushered them in for tea. Sozan told her about their recent night raid, and Rozi told them about the many successful street battles they had fought, as well as the losses of close comrades.

Nasrin said, with a cheeky grin, "The other day I said to Farhan, there were fourteen Daesh men killed when our forces attacked and destroyed a car that was fleeing."

Karin nodded, sipping her tea. Farhan sat next to her on the carpet grinning as Roza and Sozan looked confused.

"I said to him, the soldiers reported they had killed eight Daesh men, and one was wounded. I said, 'Maybe we should say nine have been killed since we don't know if he will survive." She winked at Karin. "I told him, I was only joking, and he suggested yes, maybe we should check with the doctor to see if he will pull through."

Karin laughed and looked at Farhan. "Are these the discussions you have about reporting?" she said, in a jokingly scathing manner. "Is this how you're reporting our efforts on the frontline?"

"Yes, these are our dilemmas here, Kar. A lot to consider," he said, and gave her a quick wink. Karin knew this was their way of surviving this craziness.

"Can we talk about where you think the girls are being held?" Sozan said, breaking the frivolity.

"Of course," Farhan answered, becoming more serious and looking to Nasrin.

"Yes, come over here, and we will show you on the map where the house is and the information that can hopefully help to free your sister and the women," Nasrin said.

All five of them sat down around the teapot on the cushions. A large map was spread out in front of them. Karin felt excited to think they could be closer to freeing Ashti. She welcomed the distraction from Farhan's gaze. Nasrin explained the position, the number of men believed to be guarding the women, and possible entry points into the building.

"This is the intelligence we have gained. Our guy risked his life to get close enough to work out that it was probably this house."

"Thank you so much for all of your efforts," Sozan said. "I know my sister will be so grateful to you all when we can free her. They can't do this. I want them to pay."

"We are happy to do this for you and anyone who is captured by Daesh. We hope and pray it will go well for you girls," Farhan said, looking around all of the group.

"*Zor spas*, Farhan," Rozi said.

"Will you stay to eat with us?" Farhan asked, looking only at Karin.

"Yes, please stay," Nasrin said.

Karin looked at Roza and Sozan; they both nodded, as she expected.

"Yes, we'd like that," she said.

That night they all helped to prepare the chicken that was smuggled over the border from Turkey, cutting it up in the dirt, on plates, outside the house. Later, cheese, bread, and cucumber were added. Karin knew that some of their food came from abandoned shops or was produced by the bakery that still operated in Kobane while the war raged. She knew the bakery owner, Aram, and felt proud of his efforts in staying to support the soldiers and civilians.

Cutting up the slabs of meat, she looked up at her friends all working together and paused to enjoy this moment. Karin savored this time with her friends, as no one knew what would happen in the coming weeks, days, or even the next few minutes. She resumed her chopping.

"Hey, if western journalists filmed this and didn't explain, people might think we were cutting up Daesh men," Nasrin said, laughing.

"That's very dark, Nasrin, typical of you," Karin said, laughing.

Karin looked down and tried not to notice that Farhan was looking at her for quite a while, not saying anything. In this gaze, Karin knew what he felt, but they both knew nothing would happen, not here and now. Nothing made her feel this sinking feeling in her stomach, any more, other than him. She could line up a Daesh man in her rifle and shoot him with skill and focus, but being around Farhan shot adrenalin through her veins. Karin noticed his elegant fingers as they stroked his black beard when he was considering something. But she knew she had to focus, and she would. The war wasn't over yet, not even close; she couldn't get distracted. Now, getting Sozan's sister back was the highest priority.

Inside, she felt guilt quashing her excitement for even entertaining something in this moment. It wasn't right. Mani and Ser were dead, and so many others they loved. How could she think of romance right now, standing on this windswept, barren, desert plain of a situation? Yet maybe this *was* the perfect antidote to the war, the idea of love, so civilian and 'normal', and yet, rare as well.

She remembered Commander Tolhedan saying that they must renounce conventional society, marriage, and civilian lives.

This was not an issue for Karin at the time; it was only now that she felt a tinge of desire. But it was momentary. Karin knew this, and that her inner resolve was much stronger than any other impulse.

Once they had prepared dinner, Farhan took the meat, and some of the other journalists cooked it over the stove. After they finished eating and cleaned up, they sat in their circle again. Nasrin suggested some music. One woman who Karin didn't know began to sing a song she had written after her friends had been killed. Her lone voice was thin and melancholic. It seemed to float above Karin and move around as if it expressed all of their collective emotion.

> *There were five friends in Kobane.*
>
> *They were very close.*
>
> *They couldn't stay silent while the*
>
> *Kurdish people were in danger.*
>
> *The war started in Rojava. Militants attacked us.*
>
> *Destroy the enemy and free Kurdistan!*

The group was quiet afterward; they looked into their laps and did not speak straight away. Then one called out, "Free Kurdistan! Yes." Sozan looked up from where she sat. Karin saw tears in her eyes, combined with her wide, defiant smile.

Sozan called out, "Let's dance, comrades." Everyone stood up; there were nine of them. They slung their arms over each other's shoulders and began to move in a semi-circle, kicking to the front and side. Karin was pulled into it by Roza. A bearded man in the corner began to play the *tembur*, as they started dancing with abandon moving around the small room, arm in arm, laughing loudly. Karin began to laugh too, feeling elation like she hadn't experienced since this whole battle began. She had not let her guard down for months, but now for reasons she didn't understand, she couldn't control it, and didn't want to.

She felt Farhan's warm arm over her shoulder. Being this close to him gave her an excitement she hadn't expected. Another twinge of guilt moved through her, about her ex-fiancé, Terah. She had only briefly thought about him in the past few months. He was in Iraq, fighting with the Kurdish forces. Right now, she said a silent prayer for him, and reminded herself it was over. She looked sideways at Farhan, who was laughing his deep, throaty laugh, and allowed herself to surrender to the moment. Dancing to the rhythm of the Kurdish music, in the rough semi-circle, she moved with passion and force, laughing loudly. She savored every moment of this feeling like a piece of salty and smooth goat's cheese, melting in her mouth.

- 14 -

Roza

Roza walked behind Sozan, who crouched low as she moved expertly through the holes of various building. Sozan had been on the front longer than Roza and Karin, by about two months. Her experience was evident in the easy manner in which she did all of the tasks required. Roza didn't know how Sozan managed to stay so low while maneuvering through the holes, but she continued on following her. Roza glanced back and saw Karin adjusting her weaponry as she came behind them.

Following the information they had received from Nasrin and Farhan, they had decided to act straight away, and had made this plan. Tanah was following at the rear. Roza felt unsure in her gut whether this was a real lead, but they had to pursue it. Sozan was determined, and so were Roza and Karin. They had grown up with Ashti, watching her become a woman, going from a lanky, scrawny girl with fine cheekbones, to a dignified young woman. *She was very beautiful. I mean, she* is *very beautiful,* she corrected herself. It wasn't past tense; they were going to free her and the other girls. Roza wanted this nightmare to be over. Sozan stopped ahead of her and signaled them to be quiet. Karin and Tanah moved up to where Sozan and Roza were looking out a gap in a broken window in the main room. All four of them stood to the side of the window, Roza and Karin kneeling so they could look across the narrow street. There was a fence in front of the building. It was a narrow laneway, so they were not far from the building.

Daesh men were milling around on the street, laughing and smoking. They looked on edge but were talking with high pitched voices, as if something was about to happen.

"Do you think this is it?" Sozan asked the three of them.

"It could be. How should we approach this?" Roza asked, as much to herself as the others.

"I think we need to wait, and see exactly what is happening here," Karin said.

"I agree," Tanah said.

For the next twenty minutes, they watched as men came and went from the house. Roza could tell it was killing Sozan to sit here and wait. What if her sister was in there? Some of the Daesh men were young, fifteen or sixteen years old, and she could see some were older, in their forties. The younger ones, and even the older ones, seemed unsure of what they had to do, or what they were doing; it was obvious from their gait and stance. They looked like schoolboys; Roza knew very well at high school, constantly checking if what they were doing was okay with the group, like gang members.

Some of them were scrawny, a couple of them looked like people she knew from the local market. They didn't seem as terrifying as their videos suggested. Roza had seen insecurity in these soldiers' eyes when they got close, and she had shot them. Now she saw their frantic eyes, that darted to and fro, and glanced over their shoulders constantly.

This was Roza's experience of them in combat as well. Of course, there were the gung-ho ones, that ran at them with force, hatred, and determination in their faces. It would be unwise to underestimate the bloodthirsty cruelty and barbarity of some of them. *But, most of the men are terrified we will take their hope of heaven.*

Roza had tried not to feel too much in this war, but she held so much anger and hatred inside. Her femininity cried out for these women. She herself could have been captured by Daesh. This drove Roza even harder to free these women, and with Ashti, it was even more personal. She didn't want to think of what the women were going through. *We need to do this quickly.*

There were no longer men on the street. Most had left, skulking off down the laneways, weaponry over their shoulders, all the while looking nervously around. There were a few they had counted in the building, though.

"What should we do?" Sozan asked. Roza could tell she wanted to act.

"Well, we need to get closer to see how many are in there," Roza answered.

"Okay. Maybe I should go and do some surveillance. Then we can see if we should all go over," Karin said.

"It should be me," Sozan said with determination.

"Are we sure of the number of men we have seen go inside?" Roza asked.

"We think about four. But we can't be sure," Tanah said.

"Tanah, I think you should stay here and keep watch. If anyone comes down the street, you may have to kill them."

"Okay."

"The three of us will go over. We have to assess it first if possible. We need you to back us up."

"I understand. I'll keep watch."

"Are you sure it is necessary that the three of us go?" Karin asked.

"Yes, there's four of them." Roza was determined. She didn't want to let her friends go in there alone.

"Okay, let's not deliberate anymore," Sozan said, sounding impatient now.

The three of them quietly moved towards the door, where they would let themselves out. Sozan led them out onto the road. Roza could feel every part of her body on fire with adrenalin and fear. They were exposed as they ran quietly across the street. Roza looked down the road where the Daesh men had been, but was relieved she could not see anyone. They lined up next to the fence at the front of the building. Crouching down, they crept along the stone wall and moved down the side of the sandy-colored building. Roza could hear the muffled sounds of talking and laughing as they approached. There was a window, and Sozan moved under it. Karin and Roza also positioned themselves underneath the windowsill. Roza peered up into the room. She saw four men seated on the floor; two were smoking, one was cleaning his weapon, and another one was eating.

Roza pointed to the back of the building. The others nodded. They began to move down the narrow corridor next to the building. Right at the back of the building, there was a door and a window. Karin picked up a large stone she found on the ground, and using Sozan's scarf, wrapped it in fabric. Karin moved slowly but with force and smashed the window, seeking to be as quiet as possible, knowing the men may be alerted to their presence.

She opened the door with her hand, signaling for the women to follow. Sozan was the first to follow; Roza ran in as well. They moved towards the rooms that fed off the kitchen. They heard a commotion. Sozan pointed to a shut door down the hall, and Roza followed Karin and Sozan. They entered the room; there was nothing in it. Roza's adrenalin was pulsing in her ears. Suddenly, Roza heard the loud sound of men running down the hallway. She pointed to the window on the other side of the room. They ran across the room and with the back of her machine gun, Roza smashed the window and pointed for them to go through. Immediately, she saw two black figures at the door, their eyes flashing fear and violence. She pushed Karin out of the window and began shooting at the door, watching as their bodies fell to the floor, pounded by bullets at close range. Blood appeared instantly.

"Go!" Roza pushed Sozan out as well. She continued to fire as the other two men appeared at the door. One of them began to fire as well, the bullets ricocheting plaster around Roza. She was running out of ammunition; she continued shooting and jumped out backwards, feeling lacerated by the fire. Another man fell through the door as well. There was one more that didn't appear.

The women ran down the building and across the narrow laneway. As they ran across the road, gunfire followed them. The last man was screaming from his position behind the fence. Sozan turned just before going into the building and fired at the fence. Bullets pounded the fence, and he stopped firing. Roza believed he was probably injured, but she couldn't tell. Either way, they ran into the building where Tanah was waiting her weapon pointed out of the window.

"Let's go. We don't want to wait around for more of them to come," Karin said.

Roza nodded and pushed Tanah in front of her as they continued to run now, in silence, through the buildings, until they reached safer territory. Roza knew Sozan would be disappointed.

When they finally stopped, she put her hand on her shoulder.

"We'll get them. We'll find them, no matter what."

"I hope so. The longer it goes on, I'm worried that they'll take the girls to another country and we'll never find them."

"We won't let that happen."

"Thanks, Rozi." She embraced her. Roza knew that neither of them was sure. But one thing was certain; she knew they would never give up trying.

- 15 -

Karin

A week passed since the attempt at saving the girls had failed. All of them felt disheartened that they didn't succeed. Of course, Sozan was still determined, as were Karin and Rozi. But it was hard not to feel hopeless.

"Are you sure this time, Nasrin?" Karin spoke into the phone. Nasrin reassured her on the other end about the information they had gained about the whereabouts of the captured women. They had decided to risk phone communication about this as it was important. It was always difficult because the journalists would intercept communications on Daesh radios and sometimes they received information, but it wasn't always reliable. It was difficult to make concrete conclusions from the evidence. But they had no choice but to keep pursuing different avenues. Karin couldn't afford to worry about it; she knew every lead was important. She gazed out onto the small complex of the compound.

The recent failed attempt had not diminished Karin's firm determination to find and save the girls. Now, it felt as if time was running through the glass, disappearing on them. Sozan was becoming more distressed with every day that passed. Tomorrow, they would follow up this new lead, and now Karin went inside to find Sozan, Roza, Tanah, Torani, and the Commander as well. They would plan what their strategy would be the following day.

***

When the sun rose, Karin briefly visited her sacred place on the roof and prayed for their mission that day. She felt apprehensive about it. Torani was joining them, as they needed more backup. They would travel to the Daesh occupied part of Kobane and find the address they believed was the girl's prison. Every time they attempted these rescues, in the back of her mind, Karin always worried that one of them would not come back. Then again, that was a daily reality, so this wasn't that different. However, it kept Karin awake last night and other nights, but she couldn't let it get to her. There was a mission to do; they just had to complete it. Otherwise, what fate did the women have? Ashti would be so scared. She was not fierce or strong like Sozan.

"Are we ready?"

"Yep," Sozan answered Karin, and the others nodded.

Driving through the relatively safe part of Kobane, they were being transported to an area where they would walk on foot, through and behind buildings to the destination. It took them twenty minutes to arrive in the area. They heard distant explosions, heard machine-gun fire as the frontline battles raged on nearby. The war in Kobane never stopped, not even at night.

Karin and Torani moved forward towards the building. Roza would be the sniper shot from the window and keep watch; if anyone came in, she would take them out. Sozan and Tanah were following up the rear. Karin ran across the street, keeping low, and the women followed. They lined up on the fence that stood in front of the buildings and moved towards the targeted building. The problem was that they had two back entrances, and this made everything difficult to navigate. They saw the correct building and identified the Daesh black writing on the white concrete wall out the front. Karin always felt physically sick—it was against all natural instincts to storm a building where there were people who wanted you dead.

Karin motioned to the women that she was going to go down the side of the house. Two of them would wait a little and then come. Karin and Torani led the way, pressing their back against the wall. They could hear voices, banging noises, and music playing. It was always chilling when Karin heard this, but she kept moving towards the door. She led Torani past the first door, and found a window, which did not look into the correct room. There was another door, and there was a commotion; the men were moving. Karin and Torani ducked behind an old, broken down hot-water system and turned back to signal to the other girls to not move.

The door opened, and a man came out; he looked around. He seemed to have heard something. His eyes darted around, and he came towards their hiding place. On his shoulder, he had a machine gun, but in his hand, he had a machete. Karin stopped, even her breathing, and shielded Torani behind herself. He walked past them, and Karin said some silent prayers because if he had looked even slightly to his right, he would have seen them. They both stayed perfectly still. Walking to the fence, he looked down the alleyway. Karin presumed the girls had hidden because he came straight back and passed them not noticing their bodies wedged under a table. He went back inside the door, shutting it with a loud thud. Karin looked at Torani.

"What should we do?" Torani whispered to Karin.

"Let's investigate whether they are here."

"Good idea. We may have to come back."

They both crept around the building to the back area. Looking around the wall, they saw no one. There were chairs in the back, and rubble from the bombing that was happening all the time. Big sections of concrete sat on top of itself, having been blown off nearby buildings. There was a back room; maybe this was it. Karin and Torani continued towards the room when they noticed a window. Moving closer quietly, Karin positioned herself under the window. Then she quickly looked over the sill and saw people moving around in the room; black clothing, the backs of Daesh men moving. She strained to see, and standing on her toes, she could just make out a woman's hair sitting below them. Her heart began to race. Karin did a thumbs up to Torani and pointed to the room, indicating 'they're here'. She saw another younger girl's face, bruised and battered, a man standing over her. She felt sick and enraged at the same time.

Then she saw her. Ashti was sitting on the floor, leaning against the wall. In one of those strange moments in time, Karin saw Ashti look towards the window, and their eyes met. She instantly brightened. Karin got down and began to move away from the window in case one of the men saw.

"There are many men in there. What should we do?" Torani whispered.

"We can't leave them," Karin said. "We have to get Sozan." Karin led Torani out to the street carefully, where she found Sozan and Tanah hiding behind the fence.

"We've found her."

"What?! Are you sure?"

"Yes. I saw her and she saw me."

"Really? Let's go. We have to get in there and get her."

"Wait, Sozan, let's plan first. There are many men in there. We need a plan."

"No, we don't!"

She pulled Sozan back. "I want to get her too, but we have to make sure we can get her."

They planned to distract the men in the front room and attack the men in the back room separately. Karin signaled to Roza; they needed her to come over. She crept across the street. Karin, Roza, and Torani would attack the front room, while Sozan and Tanah would wait until the men went to the front; then they would attack the rest of them, and free the girls.

Karin, Roza, and Torani crept down the side. They peered through a small window to see the number of men inside. There were five men. Roza positioned her sniper rifle in the window, knowing she had to make it precise; there was only one chance. She aimed it at the largest man sitting on the floor. Karin could see Rozi planning the following three shots after this to kill the other men. Roza smashed the glass quickly and lined up her weapon positioning the gauge on his head. She shot straight away; her target was hit and fell back instantly, a hole in his forehead. She shot the man next to him.

The men began to jump up, and as she shot a man running to get his weapon, another Daesh man started to shoot at them – Karin began firing back. Torani used a handgun as well. The sound of men running from the back of the building began to thud through to the front room. Karin signaled to Sozan pointing to the back. Sozan and Tanah ran towards the rear of the building. Just then they looked to their right. A black figure appeared, and before they knew it, he was firing, and Torani was down. Karin shot him multiple times with her handgun as she saw Torani crumpled on the ground. She was screaming. Her leg was hit, and blood was pouring out of her body. Roza continued to shoot the men appearing in the room.

"We have to go," Karin shouted. *She won't survive otherwise.*

"Okay," Roza called back over the sound of gunfire, "What about the others?"

"She will die unless we get her out of here. I'll take her across the road. You get Sozan and Tanah."

"Okay."

"Be careful," Karin said.

Karin saw Roza run to the back of the building. Karin blocked the blood that was oozing out of Torani's body, quickly checking which artery had been hit. Time was crucial now. Karin checked the wound and believed it be the femoral artery, but prayed it wasn't. She knew the femoral artery was the worst one to injure. Torani could bleed out quickly. Getting her across the road was her first priority, and then bandaging her up quickly. Karin handed Torani her shirt to hold on her wound and put her arm over her shoulder, lifting her up. She groaned with pain.

"I'll get you to safety, Tori, hang in there."

"Ah…" She groaned a little, but Karin was worried about how quiet she was.

Karin began to carry her carefully, but quickly. She didn't even know if she could help her. Her mind was racing; what was happening with the others? Gunshot could be heard, and she had no idea what was happening and who had been killed or injured. Carrying Torani across the road, Karin stumbled and nearly dropped her. Glancing back, she wanted to make sure they weren't being followed. Repositioning Torani over her shoulder, she crept along until they reached the house. Karin laid her gently on the ground, tying fabric from her shirt above the wound, tightly, to stop the blood flowing out of her. Torani was looking at Karin; she looked shocked, but also strangely peaceful. Karin sat down, cradling Torani's head in her lap. Torani touched Karin on the arm. "Thank you, dear friend."

"Stay with me, Tor. You can't…stay awake, hang on. I'm going to get help."

"You can't. I'm weak Kar…I can feel it…"

"What?" Karin felt her throat tightening.

"I'm…" Torani's voice was weak.

"No, Torani…stay awake, please…" Karin pleaded. But Torani breathed out loudly, her eyes were perfectly still, and her body went limp in Karin's arms. She was gone. Karin held her close and cried out to the empty room, "No…Torani…" as she wept.

"Now you're a martyr, sweet one, just like you always wanted, " Karin said quietly to Torani, touching her face. She held her close, wishing that Torani could laugh, tell her jokes, or smile that cheeky, rebellious smile.

Suddenly, Karin heard a commotion, and the sound of banging and people coming. She jumped up with her machine gun, ready. Sozan burst in, with Roza and Tanah and another woman.

"What happened? Where are the rest of them?"

"We couldn't get Ashti, but we freed Naza."

Sozan was looking out at the street.

"I can't leave."

"Torani died, Sozan."

"What? What do you mean?" Sozan yelled at Karin, running towards them. Roza followed. Roza stood above, looking at Torani, shocked by what had happened. Sozan knelt down next to where Karin held Torani cradled on her leg.

"I'm so sorry, Torani. Your life will not be gone for nothing. This is my fault. I need to go back in." She stroked

158

Torani's hair, gently.

"It's not your fault. Torani would want us to go back now," Karin said, "to get safe, otherwise we'll be killed. Naza can give us some information, and we'll come back for Ashti."

"I can't leave Ashti!" As Sozan said that, shooting began to pound the walls, doors, and windows and Karin jumped up.

"Let's go! I'll carry Torani."

Roza reloaded her weapon and shot out onto the street. They all began to run, with Karin in the middle of the group moving slower. After a while, the shooting stopped, and Karin had to rest. Eventually, they arrived. No one could speak. What could they say? One of the brightest girls in their group was now gone. Karin kissed Torani's forehead as she gave her body to the medics to prepare for a traditional Kurdish ceremony. They had asked if Karin and the others thought she should be buried in Kobane, as she was originally from Turkey.

Karin had answered, "Torani would want to be buried here, with her comrades." She wiped her eyes. "She was a true martyr and fought for freedom here. She would want to be buried in Kobane, where she felt the most free."

She could see Sozan was affected the most; they hadn't saved Ashti, and her friend had died in the process. Now guilt sat on her shoulders; she could see it weighing her down. She walked over to Sozan and sat down next to her in the compound. Rolling a cigarette, Karin offered it to her. Sozan took it and lit up. She held her head in her hands and did not look at Karin.

"We'll get them, I promise you," Karin said, holding her forearm firmly. She did not try to hide the tears that were falling rapidly down her cheeks.

Sozan nodded, staring straight ahead.

- 16 -

Roza

As Roza pulled up her pants, she noticed that they were loose around the middle. She had to push a new hole into her belt to keep them from falling down. Roza put her long-sleeved khaki shirt on, and smelled the diesel, smoke, and dirt on her clothes. The uniforms were only washed occasionally, by supporters of the women in Kobane.

Some who had stayed were running a small school for the children who had remained, including Yez. He had talked about it on one of their phone calls recently. She was pleased he was able to have some semblance of normality in his life. These same women would pick up the clothing from the soldiers and wash it, to be returned a day later. Roza was extremely grateful, but accepted that most of the time her clothing would be soiled. Every month the women were supplied with sanitary products obtained from across the border. This was difficult for all of them. Often, they could not even visit a toilet; rather, they had to relieve themselves in pits or holes dug out of the ground, or simply squat. Cramps knotted their stomachs here on the frontline, and yet they all pressed on.

Every month that passed, Roza experienced a strong, persistent pain that sat on top of her muscles as she lay for hours, sometimes in one position, firing her gun through a narrow hole. She reminded herself then that this was for Ser and Yez, and the freedom of her people and land. She touched her stomach. She could see Ser kissing it and laughing, and saying how much he loved it, her hand fondling his hair as he did. She had never understood why he loved her stomach and now her stomach was shrinking every day. Was she going to fade away? Not perish in a blazing fire of bullets, but simply fade gradually, every day, until she was no longer there.

Food was, at times, repugnant to Roza. She ate, but rarely felt like eating, except for when she came back from fierce fighting, then she was ravenous. The word *ravenous* made her smile. It had been the code word between herself and Sercan when they wanted each other sexually, and people were around. They would say, "Are you hungry?" and one of them would answer, "I'm ravenous." These normal words now echoed through an empty hall of nothingness and it seemed as if they were memories of a time and place that never existed. Karin walked over to her.

"Morning, Rozi."

"Hello," Roza said, as she pulled her black leather boots on, flinching with the pain of her blisters, and the fatigue of her toes from being confined every day. This pain was nothing compared to the pain she saw every day in her fellow soldiers who were injured or killed. Or the agony of when Torah was found dead, raped and dumped in the dirt. Roza had had to identify Torah after they found her body discarded in the dirt. She had seen her bruised, lacerated body and the dried blood between her thighs. Roza could never erase these images of the agony and torture Torah would have suffered before her undignified death. Torani's death last night—seeing her lifeless face, still and silent—it was wrong. She had only been 16. All of this made her feel sick most days, and sometimes she had to remind herself to breathe. Karin passed her a tin mug of black tea.

"There, this will help you wake up."

"Thanks, Kari."

She managed a smile.

"Are you feeling okay this morning, Roz?"

"I'm feeling okay," she said, touching Karin on the arm to try to reassure her. "It's just hard, you know?"

"I know."

Roza looked at Karin. They had met on the first day of their little school, held in a room in a stone building in Kobane. They had sat next to each other and ended up holding hands that day, unsure of school and this strange newness. It seemed no different now. As Roza looked at Karin they were still little girls, holding hands, facing uncertainty.

The noises of voices and clanging of metal in the makeshift kitchen, and the smell of wood fire and eggs mingling together, created a blanketing comfort. Roza moved her body mechanically out of the warmth of her scratchy grey blanket. The air was not too cold this morning. Walking into the kitchen area, Roza plonked down on a cushion on the floor. The women were getting ready around her.

"*Silav*, sis," Sozan said.

"Hi…" Roza said in a faint, croaky voice.

"Did you sleep last night?"

"Nope, not after yesterday."

"Me either," Sozan said, touching her on the shoulder as she walked past. Torani's death made Roza feel like vomiting; it hit her when she awoke after a few hours of sleep. Now, she felt a heaviness in every limb of her body. She looked around at the girls sitting on the dark mat on the floor. Some of them were loading their weapons and feeding bullets into their magazines.

Tanah was braiding Sozan's hair into tight plaits down her back. Her hair was long, light, and straight; you needed your hair out of the way during the day. She loved how Tanah and Sozan put embroidered material flowers and wove material into their hair. Even though their braids were full of dust, dirt, and gunpowder, they adorned themselves with beauty. A piece of normality woven into floral decoration as a reminder of who they hoped to be in the future; a glimpse of beauty amidst the horror, like a cool refreshing drink from a canister on the frontline. Roza said a quick prayer for protection over these women she loved. She looked at Sozan, and they exchanged knowing glances, and a slight smile.

She walked into the kitchen, and Reynaz handed her a plate with an egg and flatbread on it. Paint had peeled off the white walls of the kitchen. Pictures of female and male martyrs who had fought in the war, people they had all known, looked down on them with smiles. There was a brick stove and a black ash-covered metal plate that sat on top of an open fire to cook their meals. Metal kettles perched on the plate, brewing and bubbling; the sounds of morning tea soothed Roza.

Outside, the color of deep pink mingled with red, soothing warm orange and tentative blue, signaling the new day. Beyond the veranda, she saw the corrugated iron and tiled rooves of many buildings in this part of Kobane. She glanced at the destruction of the day before; buildings with gaping expanses, and cars flattened

164

on the dusty, white street. Everything seemed different now that Torani had died. Everything was quieter, and the girls were walking around subdued and solemn. Her bright presence was gone now; her joking, laughing, mischievous smirk, and her formidable spirit. One of the soldiers would be issued the job of contacting her relatives.

Rolling up the flatbread, she dipped it in the yolk and ate, chewing slowly, with small bites that reflected her delicate frame. Her slight body was now muscular; the small amount of fat she had had before the war was replaced with the hard sinew of defined muscle that twitched and flexed when she reloaded her weapon, taut, strong, and trained for killing. What other choice did she have? She hadn't chosen this war—it had chosen her.

Karin came over to Roza.

"Commander Beritan has instructions for us to go to the Cultural Centre. We have to go," Karin said.

Roza and Karin moved into the operations room at the back of the building. After seating herself, Roza listened to the Commander explain different elements of the operation, and where some of the women soldiers would be situated. The Commander turned to Roza.

"Today, I want you, Karin, Sozan, and Tanah to be closer down here; we need to target their base in the Tishrin School."

Commander Beritan pointed to it on the map.

"Reynaz, Aster, Josef, and Ahmed will be fifty meters to your right."

"Yes, Commander," Roza answered. Roza and Karin went and found the others; they were loading their ammunition and strapping their bullet belts across their chest.

"The position is a bit more exposed this time, girls," Roza said to Karin and Sozan. Tanah was standing a little further off. Roza hoped the Commander knew what she was doing; this position seemed quite risky.

"Yes, I've seen it. We'll have to be more vigilant there, okay? It's closer to the enemy, and we need to be careful."

"Definitely," said Sozan. She looked up from her weapon and nodded. She had an ability to be very serious while having a slight smirk lurking in the corners of her smile. Sozan had always been like this, ever since Roza met her that day in high school where she first saw her smile, quiet but somehow bold behind the reserve. Sozan had always been more daring than the other girls, breaking the rules about talking to men, wearing jeans and t-shirts, and going without a headdress, as she wasn't Islamic. She even smoked before the others did; her mother had told her she was not being 'a true Kurdish girl.' Sozan had laughed and asked, "What is a Kurdish girl like, Mami?"

All together they made their way further down the hill. The other soldiers were higher up, and as they walked, they began to feel the isolated position of this post. Roza felt vulnerable moving towards their post, but silenced her doubts by reminding herself she trusted the Commander. *She must've weighed this up, surely.* Sozan walked next to Roza and pulled her into a strong embrace. Roza reciprocated even with their weaponry and guns they managed to hug. She felt the sickness in her stomach easing. Sozan always had this effect on Roza.

"How are you coping, sis?"

She put her arm around Roza; her voice was serious.

166

"As good as can be, I guess. I feel sick. You?"

"Me too. I feel angry about Torani and Ashti."

"Me too," Roza put her arm around Sozan in return, and squeezed her to acknowledge the pain she must be going through.

"Women, freedom, life," Sozan said to Roza.

"Yes, sis," Roza replied. She could hear the weariness in Sozan's voice and felt the same.

They reached the section that had been prepared for them with sandbags and a small wall made of large boulders pushed together. When they noticed movement of the figures dressed in black, only a few hundred meters away in the single-story school building, they crouched down quickly.

All of the girls sought to quickly set up their tripods for their machine guns, but before they finished, gunfire had started, relentless and hard. Bullet fire pounded the sandbags, bursting them open. Roza grabbed her gun and began shooting; she saw her bullets smashing holes in the windows of the white building. Sozan and Karin began firing as well. Then all four of the women responded with a cacophony of fire.

Suddenly, there was an explosion just next to their cover; it blew sections of the wall up, sending shards of concrete and stone outward. Tanah ducked behind Karin as she was exposed. Another explosion came rapidly not far from them, exploding dust and rocks through the air. Dust obscured their sight. Roza couldn't see, but kept firing straight ahead. The black figures now seemed to be advancing towards them. Roza heard the men screaming and yelling, and she could almost make out their faces. Her eyes began to water, and she blinked it away, as she saw them sprinting towards them. Adrenalin filled her whole body, and she could barely breathe.

"Pull back!" Roza yelled to the others. "Pull out, let's go!"

She jumped up from her position and grabbed Karin. Tanah jumped to her feet as well. They began to run. Sozan called to them, "I'm staying! Go!"

Roza called to her through the confusion, "No! Retreat! Retreat!"

Sozan held out her hand with the small green grenade in it. She made the sign of the cross across her chest. The men were now only ten meters away. Karin pulled both Roza and Tanah up the hill, yelling, "Run!" Roza began to run, looking back once. She saw Sozan's face briefly, the flash of her eyes; then the explosion of fire, rocks, dirt, a huge cloud, and a wall of heat that forced them to the ground. Roza looked back. There were men dead on the ground, but she could not see Sozan. Karin scooped Roza up, as she had fallen to the ground. Roza pulled Tanah, and they ran through the darkening streets, for what seemed like the longest time, until they reached the compound. As they entered, the soldiers fired outwards in case they had been followed.

Roza doubled over. Holding her knees, she vomited clear fluid everywhere. She sobbed breathlessly, and kept saying, "Sozan, Sozan, Sozan…" like a mantra to herself, over and over.

- 17 -

Karin

Karin sought to savor the smooth texture and flavor of a cube of Kurdish cheese in her mouth as she added potato and olive oil. She wanted to suppress how she was feeling from the devastation of Sozan's loss. Before all the women was a spread of chicken, from over the border, and flatbread from Aram's bakery. The garlic, olive oil and rich herbs mingled perfectly into the savory chicken. Pots of tea sat on the floor with them. Karin dipped her flatbread into the olive oil; it made her think of Maia. She would give anything right now to taste her mother's dolma and traditional Kurdish cooking.

Reynaz and Tanah whispered next to Karin. Roza sat silently on Karin's left. She noticed Roza wasn't eating.

"You hungry, Rozi?" Karin asked. Roza shook her head.

Karin had tried to comfort Roza earlier, but she had not wanted to talk. Roza had disappeared after getting back to the compound. She was obviously devastated about Sozan, as Karin was. But how could they process this? Their closest friend blowing herself up to save them. Karin knew Roza preferred to be alone when she was feeling and thinking a lot. The truth was, she didn't know what to say. This was the first time in their friendship she had felt a distance between herself and Roza, even considering the conflict they had experienced about Ser initially. But this was different. It was more unnerving; it felt as if she was losing Roza. A week ago, they had lost Torani, and now Sozan was dead. Karin felt it, of course, she did, but she suppressed her emotions to keep going. She was afraid if she let herself feel it, she would not be able to go on.

Right now, she felt she had no more tears to cry, and couldn't swallow. As much as she wanted to enjoy the food in front of her, she couldn't. When she closed her eyes, she kept seeing the moment over and over, the terrifying screams of the men as they had run towards them, the roar of the explosion, fire blazing into an immense cloud, intense heat, being thrown through the air. Sozan's face. The images were as relentless as the daily bombing and shellfire.

"It was a terrible thing that happened today. Losing Torani a few days ago and now, Sozan. May they rest in peace now," Commander Beritan said, looking directly at Karin and Roza. The Commander's eyes had tears. Karin saw that Roza did not raise her head.

"Yes, it was. Yes, may *Xwa* keep them," Karin answered her. Karin looked at her metal plate of food, and suddenly felt sick. The Commander's acknowledgment, though comforting, brought everything into the present, as if another horrifying entity now sat at their mealtime. She felt something at the back of her throat, large and unyielding.

"Sozan was a true warrior. May her God give her rest," Reynaz said from the other side of the circle.

"Yes, may she rest with God," Tanah said, quietly crossing her chest with a down and across motion. "She sacrificed herself for us. She was so brave." Tanah continued.

Roza stood up and said, "Excuse me."

The Commander nodded, and Karin could see her face furrowed with concern for Roza. Karin watched Roza walk out onto the small veranda. She stood up and followed.

Roza was sitting on the ground, knees bent up close to her chest, and her arms draped across them. She faced out into the twilight, the colors darkening and deepening in the distance, hanging over the buildings. Karin couldn't see her face. Roza's shoulders looked smaller and more fragile than Karin had ever seen before.

"I can't listen to that and be in there," Roza said. "Sozan had her whole life ahead of her and now..."

"I know. They're just acknowledging our pain and Sozan's sacrifice."

"I know, but Kar..." Roza turned and faced her. "I'm so angry. I didn't want her to sacrifice herself for me; she could've run. Kar, she should've run."

Karin could see Roza was crying.

"I know," Karin said. She moved towards her friend and put her arm around her.

"I have so much anger burning inside. I can't take any more loss." Roza hid her face in her hands. Karin embraced her, saying nothing. Tears began to form in Karin's eyes and fall down her cheeks. Her throat ached. It was difficult to see Roza like this, her closest friend, to lose Sozan and Torani and then see Roza suffering as well. This was all too much.

"She sacrificed herself for us. I can understand that. I would've done the same thing." Karin said.

Roza turned and faced her.

"Don't ever do that for me."

"I would, in a second," Karin said in a quiet tone. "Sozan died with dignity."

"You don't seriously believe that, do you?" Roza asked. Her voice was loud and strained. "There's no dignity in this bloody war; everyone dies in the dirt." She turned away from Karin.

"I know, but we're fighting for Kobane. That's more important than our lives."

Roza didn't say anything for a few moments.

"I know," Roza said eventually. "But sometimes, I can't take it. Maybe I should take Yez and my family and leave?"

"You don't regret staying, do you? We are so close to victory, Roz. We did the right thing."

"No, I don't regret fighting," she said. "After Ser died, I didn't have any other choice. I wasn't going to wait until they came to kill us. But I'm wondering if I should take Yez out now."

"I understand. I wouldn't blame you if you did this."

"I feel such an emptiness being separated from him now; it's unbearable."

"I understand," Karin answered, taking out a cigarette.

Roza turned back towards Karin.

"I don't think you do. How could you? You don't have any children. You have no idea how I feel; as if one of my limbs has been severed from my body. Do you have any idea how that feels?"

"I do know how you feel; my brother was killed like an animal. You don't think that's horrendous enough?"

"I know you've suffered, but it's different when it's your child. I can't help feeling alone, like you don't understand. Sometimes, I wonder if you've always secretly resented me marrying and having Yez. You seemed jealous when I got to know Ser, always sulking. Maybe it's because you really wanted to marry Terah and you resented that I got married. I got married *and* studied. You had to choose between him and medicine. That's not my fault."

"I was happy for you," Karin said, shocked. "I didn't resent you. Of course, I *was* hurt about Terah, but what choice did I have? I had to be myself and pursue my purpose. Where's this coming from?"

"I feel so alone right now, Kar. And Sozan's gone…"

"You're not the only one in pain, Roza. I lost her too. I can't believe she's gone. It feels like you blame me for being here. I always wanted to be here, but you didn't…"

173

Roza turned to Karin; her face was red and blotchy.

"I don't blame you. You weren't the reason I joined the fight... They were." She pointed outwards into the darkening afternoon.

"I don't want her life to be lost for nothing." Roza wept bitterly and hid her face in her hands.

"Me, too, Rozi, me, too."

Silence sat between them; it felt heavy. They both looked out into the distant skies. Karin wished she was a child again, losing herself in climbing the spindly branches of the olive trees on their farm. She felt the cool air under the olive tree now, and the sunset shot pink, blue, and deep maroon across the horizon. It almost seemed irreverent to Sozan's death, an oblivious display of beauty in the face of pain. The sun should be eclipsed, and the sky blood-red. It was almost unbearable to gaze upon this splendor.

After a while, Karin reached out and put her arm around Roza. Roza buried her face into Karin's shoulder, her body shook, and she wept. Karin wept also; their bodies were as if one, and they held each other up under the weight of their shared devastation.

***

In their usual meeting with the whole battalion of fifty women, Beritan announced that they would soon have a journalist visiting from Australia. Sarah Johns was her name; and she was making a feature for a program on a station called ABC. She was to stay for a few days in total. The Commander asked for a volunteer to look after her. No one did. No one wanted the distraction or annoyance of a journalist.

Tanah put up her hand.

"You volunteering, Tanah?"

"No, Commander. I think Karin and Roza should do it. They have by far the best English of all of us."

"Yes, true." Beritan looked over at Karin, who was surprised by the suggestion and didn't know what to say. She glanced at Roza next to her, shrugging her shoulders as a question to Roza.

Roza looked irritated by the suggestion.

"Yes, I think it would be a good break for you two, from everything," Beritan said, directly addressing them. "Sarah will be arriving in a day. After visiting us, she will move on to the journalists that are here in Kobane. We all know them."

Beritan smiled at the soldiers. Karin turned to Roza; she was not happy and looked down at her lap. After the meeting broke up, the Commander approached Karin.

"I do think it's a good idea for you to take care of the journalist. You two need a break. You have been through such a trauma, and we're all feeling the loss of Sozan. She was such a wonderful person. I miss her." The Commander looked down. Karin had never seen her affected by anything.

"I want you to have a rest from battle for a few days, and Sarah will be a good way for you to do this."

"Okay, I appreciate that. Roza is definitely suffering about Soz."

"She is. But you need to let yourself grieve as well, Kar."

"Thanks, Commander. I will." Karin didn't feel completely comfortable talking to the Commander about this. She wanted to find Roza and see how she was.

"We'll look after Sarah, no problems, and keep her safe," Karin assured the Commander. She felt irritated at having to do this right now; she wanted to focus on her promise to Sozan to save Ashti. *If the journalist didn't want to be in danger, she shouldn't have come here*. She had been through this with journalists before. There had been a man-and-woman team from somewhere in Eastern Europe; they had an air of superiority, and were more concerned with their appearance on camera than covering the conflict.

There had been press from the UK who came and took a series of photographs, making them pose with guns, and focused on the women's appearance instead of the war. The article's angle, discovered later by the Commander, was in effect, 'Look at these hot women soldiers.' Karin was disgusted. Her friends were losing their lives every day, and these outlets were objectifying them. No wonder she and Roza were wary of Western journalists. It made her angry when she thought of Nasrin and Farhan and the other local journalists who remained in Kobane. They risked their lives every day to report from within the war. She was incensed at the vanity of some of the journalists who were more concerned with being seen to cover the war, than actually engaging and telling their stories. Karin left to find Roza. She was concerned for her, but another nagging sensation also sat in her stomach: her promise to save Ashti. Her anger was channeled into this promise, and she wanted to talk to Roza and the Commander about the plan. This was what kept her going right now; this was her oxygen. She felt numb in a way, like her body and soul had transformed into a machine, but she knew what she had to do now. Sozan's death would not be in vain.

***

Sarah Johns walked into the room with a cameraman shouldering his equipment. Karin noticed how Sarah stood with her shoulders back, walking with a casual, confident stride, her legs long and slim, seeming to lead the way for her upper body. Her presence in the room, strangely, was both unassuming and commanding at the same time. Her frame did, however, slump forward somewhat in a posture of weariness. Her hair was short and dark like a raven's; her eyes were a green Karin had rarely seen, deep in color, with light inflections towards the pupil and framed by long, black eyelashes. She was not wearing makeup and wore khaki pants and a black t-shirt that hung over her pants.

In her childhood, Karin remembered, her family had encountered an Australian couple who were traveling through Syria. They had worn jeans, t-shirts, colorful beanies, and woolen jackets, and said they were 'exploring the Middle East.' Karin had never encountered a female like this girl. She was warm and smiled a lot, and had a loud laugh that filled the air between them; she couldn't remember her name. The couple had wanted to work on the family's olive farm, but Aster couldn't do it. He didn't understand why they would want to do this. He had taken them in for a meal and told them he did not have anything to offer them. Karin remembered feeling both scared and intrigued by the couple, wondering what this place Australia they spoke of was like, where the women traveled across the world with their partners and did not wear wedding rings or headscarves. Later Karin discovered, when she studied at Damascus University, that there were many Kurdish people in Australia. She began to wonder what it was like to live there. Looking at the landscapes in Australia, she noticed there were many deserts, like Kobane, but also forests and coastlines. But she knew she could never leave Kobane.

Karin did not look directly at the man accompanying the journalist, though she was curious about what an Australian man might look like. She glanced over at him with quick, timid looks to take in his features. He seemed to meander and want to slip in unnoticed. It looked like he was comfortable with the fact that he always followed Sarah into the room. Karin felt amused. He seemed to be like a leather handbag for Sarah, but not the ornamental kind; the kind that is essential, practical, and even life-saving.

He was tall, and also wore khaki army pants, and a baggy red t-shirt. He looked somewhat similar to Kurdish men actually, which surprised Karin. He had dark eyes and eyebrows. It was the way he walked and held himself that was different. He occupied space in the room as if he was simultaneously a part of the fabric of the room, blending in, but also completely at ease; as if he had lived in Kobane his whole life. *I guess that is what happens when you travel the world into conflict...everywhere is your home.* This thought was completely foreign to Karin. She could not begin to comprehend it. Karin sat on a cushion on the colorfully patterned tapestry rug. Sarah came and sat directly in front of her on the floor, crossing her legs. She placed her tape recorder and notebook down and made space for her cameraman, then smiled at Karin.

"*Silav. Navé min* Sarah e." She extended her hand out to Karin. Karin shook it, knowing this was her custom. Turning to the man beside her, she said, "This is Marcel." He smiled and nodded at Karin.

"*Silav*, I'm Karin." Karin was surprised that this woman knew a little Kurmanji Kurdish.

"Thanks very much for agreeing to talk to me. The Commander told me you lost your friends recently. I'm very sorry for your loss. Sozan and Torani, I believe?"

"Yes, we did. Thank you," Karin said.

Sarah adjusted her wristwatch, which had a wide brown leather band and large numerical face. *Most people don't wear watches anymore.*

"We can wait until tomorrow to do more reporting. Thank you so much for agreeing to show us around, and talking to me about the situation."

"Thank you very much for coming here," Karin said in a dull tone, hoping her English was understandable. She had studied it her whole life, and also studied with English speakers at university.

"I'll take you around tomorrow," she said. "Tonight, you'll sleep in our base. You'll be safe."

"Thanks so much," Sarah said, smiling at Karin. Karin couldn't help but notice, on the edges of her mouth, a mischievousness not entirely muted by the situation.

- 18 -

Roza

Roza sat against the wall of the lounge room on a cushion, cleaning her gun. Using a toothbrush, Roza worked in the crevices and gaps of the parts of the AK 47 shaft, removing small dirt particles out of the magazine. Every few days she cleaned her weapon. She enjoyed the rhythmical motion of polishing the wood and metal.

She felt closer to Karin after clearing the air last night. She couldn't be in this war without her. After Sozan and Torani's deaths, Roza had felt weaker than usual. Something had become dark around her; a nagging feeling that everything was futile plagued her. A craving to see Yez was becoming overwhelming for her now. His innocence, warmth, the young, optimistic life in him…this was all she wanted now. She had had enough of blood - filled violence, gore, and loss; she couldn't take anymore.

Since the day that Sozan died, she hadn't been able to eat even a small amount of food. At one point, she felt her legs collapse beneath her, and Tanah had had to assist her. Holding the weight of her weapon, she looked at it as an instrument of power and liberty in this chaos. Roza held it with pride, though she wished she didn't have to use it at all. For the first time since joining the resistance, Roza was seriously considering leaving and returning to Yez.

"Roza," Karin said, as she touched her shoulder.

Roza turned around and said, "Hi" to the Western woman standing with Karin. This was obviously the journalist Karin had mentioned. Roza felt irritated, though she wasn't sure why; but it felt like an intrusion at the moment.

"*Silav.* Navé *min,* Sarah e, good to meet you," she said.
"*Silav.* I'm Roza."

Sarah reached out to shake Roza's hand.

"*Chawa ye?*" Sarah asked.

"I'm alright, thank you," Roza answered, impressed by Sarah's use of Kurdish despite herself.

"Karin has told me some of what you have been through recently and what's happening at the moment. I hope you don't mind, today I'll be around you both. I want to report everything you're doing and the victories you've been having. It's amazing what you've achieved here."

"Thank you very much," Roza said in a subdued manner, still feeling wary of the stranger.

"Roza, can I speak to you for a minute?" Karin asked her, signaling for them to move away.

"Sarah wants to see everything—she even said she wanted to see the Daesh men that were killed today. What do you think?"

"Is she sure she can handle it?"

"She's covered wars, Roz. They don't send a novice to a war like this," Karin said with a slight irritation in her voice.

"I know. But, still, do you think it is a good idea?"

"Yes, it'll be okay. She said she wants to see everything, even if it's grotesque."

"Ok, well I'll go along with whatever you decide. We can show her how everything is operating as well."

"That's a good idea."

Roza and Karin armed themselves and led Sarah and Marcel to the sandy earth a kilometer from their base. As they approached the area, the stench of death filled Roza's nose, its pungent, repulsive scent of decaying flesh consumed by minuscule animals and bacteria. It reminded Roza of when her dog was found dead in the field near their house. The scent had been dense and sweet, with an edge that made her feel like vomiting if she inhaled too deeply. It assaulted her senses now. She put her scarf up to her nose, as did Karin, Sarah, and Marcel.

Roza walked along the line of dead men, moving ahead of the others, as she didn't want to be filmed. She felt some relief at the sight of these men, knowing they had been stopped; however, she wanted to look at them individually, to see their faces, to acknowledge their humanity. She wanted to do this without making conversation or answering questions. Though these bodies were the enemy, Roza wanted to give them some dignity.

Walking slowly past them, she saw their legs were spread apart in various ways. One or two of them looked peaceful as if they were asleep, and a few of them had their eyes still open. She could not help herself; holding her scarf on her face, she reached down and closed their eyes with the care of a relative. Looking at their faces, she noticed some of them had sharply defined noses, and others had finely formed cheekbones and full eyebrows. She could not help but think of Ser, Mani, and, of course Yez. Karin was talking to Sarah about the details of how these bodies came to be in this temporary place before burial.

Her thoughts turned to their mothers, fathers, brothers, sisters, or wives—and to Sozan. She stopped in front of one of them. His nose was a lot like Sercan's; his face looked familiar, like someone from childhood. She could not dwell here. These men had fingers and toes; she looked down at her hands and fanned out her fingers. She had long, strong nails and elegant fingers.

Roza felt torn between the desire to fight for Kobane and her growing urge to flee with Yez. Things almost seemed hopeless to her now, after Sozan's death. Sozan could always make Roza feel lighter after she had suffered violence from her uncle. She was the only one of her close friends who understood what it felt like to experience it. Sozan had suffered it for years from her father. When Roza would come to school concealing a black eye with makeup, Sozan would make jokes about men so weak they had to pick on teenage women. She would embrace Roza and show her she was not alone, and that none of it was her fault. If Roza hadn't had this, she could not have survived that long-ago personal hell. *I wish you were here, Soz. Why did you leave me?* Roza said these things silently, hoping that Sozan could hear her.

Looking at the men lined up like this, she felt death breathing down on them every day, as close as a person next to them. Like Sozan's death. These men would not get an official burial. Inside her now, as she passed them silently, she sought to give them a symbolic ceremony. At the same time, she felt enraged that these men had placed herself, her family, community, and this whole region into an intimate dance with death and decay. This did not mean she would put down her weapon or stop the fight against these men; it simply gave her a sadness deeper than she had realized, like looking down a well of blackness, where no light permeates. Though Roza felt an internal weariness, she sought to summon her resolve by imagining Ser, and how they used to walk down the street hand in hand. She couldn't give up; otherwise, his death, and that of Sozan, Torani, and Mani were for nothing. Victory seemed closer every day. She knew every morning she faced death. This ugly apparition could be her future. She was prepared, and felt at least she would be reunited with Ser, Sozan, and Torani. But she would have to leave Yez forever, and this was so abhorrent, she couldn't bear to think about it. Sozan's eyes appeared before her and then vanished.

"Can we go, please?" Roza asked Karin, who was walking behind her with Sarah in silence.

"Yes, Roz."

Roza walked briskly in the other direction, sensing that the others did not want to stay any longer either. She led the group through the open area of dirt, and they moved towards a street with jagged pieces of building in rectangular formations, strewn across smashed concrete. It wasn't long before they reached the makeshift YPJ martyr's graveyard. The Kobane Cemetery was under Daesh control. This felt like home for Roza. This was where four people she loved lay, and her most precious person, Ser. This was Roza's sacred place, and would always be.

Stretching for fifty meters, all that could be seen were large mounds of dirt. Flowers and photographs had been placed on some, and on others cement blocks held up roughly-drawn labels on paper with names and tributes to the people lost.

"Are Sozan and your other loved ones buried here?" Sarah asked in a soft voice.

"Yes, Sozan's grave is over here," Roza replied. "Our friend Torani is over there as well. We couldn't bury Sozan's body, but we buried a few of her things here for her family to visit."

Roza pointed to a fresh mound of dirt. She did not want to take Sarah to see Ser's grave; this was too sacred for her, too personal. Even taking her to see Sozan's grave was not that comfortable, but it was preferable. On top of the grave, were two pink and red roses, placed by Tanah the day before. Roza led the way to the grave, slowly and with some hesitation. She didn't know if she wanted to be here at this place with this stranger. Ser's grave was just beyond Sozan's and Torani's; there was too much sorrow here. Why did this journalist want to be here? *These are our people.* Sarah and Karin followed. Roza stopped in front of the grave; she knelt down and gently patted the dirt near the photo of Sozan. Sarah didn't come close. Tanah had placed the 'Lord is my Shepherd' passage from *Psalms* onto the grave. Tanah knew Sozan would like it. Roza didn't understand Sozan's Christian faith, but she respected it. She couldn't move, and just bowed her head.

"I'll give you some time," Sarah said, nodding to Marcel.

They both moved away. Karin moved close to Roza and put her arm around her shoulder. They did not speak, but both knelt, closed their eyes, raised their hands in cup-like formation facing the sky, and bowing their heads, prayed. Tears rolled down Roza's face, but it felt good to be here, to feel close to Sozan, and with Karin's strength next to her, she felt comforted.

After what seemed a long time, Roza pulled herself up out of the dirt. She helped Karin up as well. They both walked towards Sarah and Marcel. Roza briefly looked back at the grave and Sozan's picture. As they left Roza, blew a kiss towards Ser's grave; she would come back privately to visit him. Then she turned to see that Karin and Sarah were walking side by side, and Marcel was close behind. Roza signaled that they should stay near the buildings, and not walk in the middle of the dusty, dirt road, towards the YPJ-secured part of Kobane.

Suddenly, from one of the darkened alleys, three ducks came waddling out in front of Roza, making a lot of loud, deep croaky noises. Sarah was delighted to see them, and laughed. She motioned to Marcel to film the ducks, moving down a street of war. One of the ducks was white with an orange beak; one was brown with a jade green head, and beautiful patterns on its feathers; and the last one had stripes of brown and speckled patterns in beige. Roza watched how they moved along, oblivious and lost.

"Chh, chh, chh, chh," Roza said to the ducks, getting them to move along, and guiding them into the nearest yard, relieved they didn't have any young with them. The ducks quacked with a throaty bark, sounding like the snorting of someone blowing their nose as they moved further into the yard of a house damaged by the war.

***

187

After returning from the cemetery, Roza, Karin, and Sarah sat on the veranda at the base, with a pot of tea in front of them and small porcelain teacups with no handles. Roza sipped her tea as Sarah began to ask some questions. Marcel was filming all three of the women, and Sarah had a tape-recorder sitting on the concrete between them.

"I need to ask something that I don't understand fully," Sarah said. "I understand why Daesh hates Christians or atheists or people in opposition to their religion, but I don't get why ISIS, or Daesh, who are Sunni, are killing other Sunnis like you as well."

Karin looked at Sarah and examined her momentarily.

"This is a complicated question which many in the West will find confusing," Karin said. "Think about how your Catholics and Protestants used to kill each other; it is similar in Islam. It's true that Daesh and the Kurds both are under the Sunni banner. Well, Daesh claims to be. However, many scholars say Daesh does not fall under the Sunni doctrines. They follow what is called Wahhabism, which claims to be seeking to purify Islam."

Sarah nodded, to show that she was following.

"A man named Muhammad ibn Abd al-Wahhab from eastern Arabia propagated this belief in the 18th century," Karin continued. "He wrote his beliefs in a book, *Al-Tawhid*, and died in 1791. He was building on the beliefs of another Islamic teacher, called Ibn Taymiyyah, from the 14th century, who was prosecuted in Turkey and executed for his beliefs.

"Following the creation of Shiites as supporters of another aspect of Islam after Mohamed died, a sect called the Khawarij formed. They disagreed with Sunni and Shiite doctrine. Their beliefs were violent; they murdered people who disagreed with them, and there were a lot of violent struggles between Sunnis and Shiite sects following this. But a more recent sect is Wahhabism, which combines beliefs from Khawarij and the Mujassimah sects who believe that God is like human beings. Wahhabism claims they are trying to purify Islam. They call themselves 'Salafi', meaning 'a thing that existed before.'" Karin stopped, clearing her throat, then looked at Sarah and started speaking again.

"Al-Wahhab viewed grave visits and tomb buildings, as well as Mawlid-reading, Sufism, *mimbar* and the minaret in the mosques, and using prayer beads for prayers, a disgrace to the religion of Islam. This is why they destroy monuments or tombs, and museums and other things. They see other Sunni Muslims as disgracing Islam, and think they need to be corrected using force. Respected Islamic scholars do not regard Wahhabism as part of being a Sunni Muslim; they do not hold the same views. So, when you say we are both of Sunni Muslims, this is not actually correct. It is very difficult for an outside person to understand this level of complexity," Karin said, looking over to see Roza's response. Roza was nodding.

"Yes, you're right about the complexity it is difficult for an outsider," said Sarah. "That does make sense… Thanks for explaining that. I'll have to do more research to fully understand the intricacies of what you just said. Thanks a lot, Karin." Sarah laughed and looked down at her notes "I need to learn a lot more about this conflict, I realize now. " Sarah shot Marcel a look as if for reassurance.

"But it does explain how Daesh justifies their violence towards other Muslims," Sarah said.

Karin nodded. "It justifies itself in their minds, but has no basis in Sunni Islam," she said, emphatically.

"I understand," Sarah replied. "It must be hard to be fighting other Muslims, though."

"It is. But we have no choice."

"Let's talk about what you've been doing in this war," Sarah said. "In fighting for Kobane, those who defended this city were majority female troops, correct?"

"Yes, the majority of the troops here are female," Roza said, finally entering into the conversation.

"And the battle has been making significant progress, pushing Daesh back fifty kilometers, which is amazing, due to your tireless fighting. I know you follow the ideals of Abdullah Ocalan—and your forces present the largest number of women fighting here in the YPJ. My question is: are you, as well as fighting Daesh, also seeking to start a revolution?"

"Yes," said Karin. "We're fighting for the rights of women, as much as fighting for our land. We've been fighting for our land for many years now. We are fighting tyranny, patriarchy, and barbarism."

"I must say you both have good English and seem very well-educated. Have you been to university? Is that common in your area, or do women suffer in terms of education?"

"In some areas, yes. But actually we, as Kurds, believe in education for everyone. I studied medicine until the war stopped my final exams, and Roza studied English Literature at Damascus University. Yes, it is a misconception that we're not all educated, though I don't blame people from the West thinking these things. Indeed, some women in these regions do not have access to education; that is a violation of our rights."

"Ah, I see," said Sarah, "that's very interesting. Roza, you've been very quiet. Can you tell me why you joined the fight?"

"Yes, well, my family stayed in Kobane, as my husband was fighting Daesh. They are still in Kobane in the safe section. Then my husband was killed fighting Daesh, and I felt I had to do something," Roza said. "I didn't want Daesh to come and kill all of us. I also wanted to defend our land for Yez. He lost his father; I couldn't let him lose that as well. It's our place, our identity. So, it was for my husband and for my son's future and our land. I was angry. I can't help it, and its growing and now with the death of my friends…"

She looked away. "I would die for them if I had to."

"Do you worry about your son?" Sarah asked.

"Yes, all the time," Roza replied quietly. "We ring our families sometimes, but we know they are safe right now. We know what is going on and we check up all the time on them."

"That's good… I'm glad to hear that," Sarah said, nodding.

Roza felt her cheeks heat up. It felt like this stranger was judging her, questioning her about Yez. She had an urge to get up and walk away, but she didn't. What did this woman know? Did she know how her people felt? Did she know how much they had struggled to gain this land? Did she know that the death of Roza's husband had created a chasm inside her that made her feel as if she was being hollowed out and dying? Did Sarah know what it was to be Kurdish? To want to be safe in a homeland, and recognized as a people? Roza didn't think so. She did not want to sit here responding to questions about why she had left Yez to take-up arms in this bloody battle she despised.

Noticing Roza's discomfort, Sarah said, "I don't mean to pry, Roza. I understand this would have been extremely difficult." Roza looked at Sarah's large green eyes and saw in the soft lines around her mouth a tenderness she had not noticed. On Sarah's neck, Roza saw there were pink blotches as if she had been clutching her skin. Roza realized Sarah was, quite likely, very anxious being here.

"*Zor spas*," Roza said quietly, looking down into her lap and forgetting to speak in English.

***

Later that night, they were all sitting around the fire. The men were laughing, and they were all talking amongst themselves. Fire danced between them; it illuminated their faces now and then. It felt good to be sitting and resting. Roza looked at Karin and smiled.

"It's so hypocritical, hey?"

192

"What?"

"We found drugs, again today, on the Daesh men, and yet they say they are against that."

"Yes, so many contradictions, hey? They claim to be Muslim and yet destroy our mosques." Karin put her arm around Roza and hugged her.

"Yeah, we're infidels. At least we're driving them out now."

"Yes." Roza looked into the fire. "They totally underestimate us, don't they?"

"Which is excellent for us, then we pounce," Karin said, mimicking a cat on the prowl. She laughed. Music began to play, filling the night air with beauty and a soothing sensation like the feeling of silk on her skin. Some of the men began to dance, as did the women. Roza smiled and stood up. Despite her weariness, she began to dance. She linked arms with the other women as they moved as one single entity, kicking their legs out to the fast Kurdish music.

- 19 -

Karin

The following morning, Karin ducked down and moved through the large hole in the wall of the building, signaling for the others to follow. Sarah followed, with Marcel behind her and Roza at the rear. Holes the size of doors had been blown out of building interior walls by the soldiers all along the street. This allowed people and soldiers to move down the streets of Kobane without risking their lives from snipers.

"This is ingenious," Sarah said, as she ducked through the gap in the rough concrete.

"Yes, it has saved a lot of us from fire on the streets," Karin answered.

Karin glanced back, saw Roza coming through as well, and smiled at her. She had told Roza she would take the lead today. She led the small group through the lounge room of this house. It had small round, holes in its walls, wallpaper peeling off, cushions strewn across the concrete floor, and a Persian rug crookedly positioned on the ground. Small stuffed toys were maimed and abandoned on the floor; a blue donkey lay on its face with dirt all through its fur. Books were splayed out on the floor. They moved through this house and the next two in silence.

Moving through another hole in the wall, Karin felt apprehensive, though she didn't know why. As she came through, she heard footsteps and movement. She grabbed her weapon and slung it over her shoulder. She motioned for the others to pause as she moved through cautiously. Stepping into the room, she heard a sound to the left of them, movement and rustling. Her heart began to race. Karin crept cautiously across the floor to approach the door to the next room. Could Daesh have infiltrated into their buildings? She moved quietly along the wall. The others were still waiting in the other building. Moving carefully towards the opening between the rooms, she peered around the edge of the door.

Suddenly, she saw two people coming towards her, one of them yelled.

"I'll shoot!"

Just as quickly, she saw the face of an older man with a white beard and next to him, a lady with darker grey hair. Both of them were armed.

Karin quickly raised her hands into the air. She came out slowly.

"We are friends, comrades," she called to them. As she came into full view, she saw that they both had guns, one was a rifle and the other a hunting gun. They were both pointing their guns towards Karin. When they realized she was from the YPJ, they lowered their guns. The lady looked relieved, as did the older man.

"*Silav*, I'm Karin."

"Good to meet you," the woman said. "I'm Bezna, and this is Ardan. We have been defending our place, just as you are."

She motioned to Karin's weaponry. "We are using a hunting gun we already had, and also one of our friends gave us this shotgun."

"Well, that's good that you can arm yourselves, and *Zor spas*. You're both very brave," Karin said.

Karin went back and retrieved the others who were peering through to see what was happening. She explained to Sarah that these people had joined the resistance, and that there were many people like them who had stayed to defend Kobane. Sarah looked impressed, and interviewed them briefly to find out their story and how the battle had been for them. Karin and Roza waited, listening to the story of how this couple had lost their son and daughter in the conflict, but how they would not give up.

Bezna was a formidable woman. Karin could tell she was strong, even with her small frame. She wore a floral pink headscarf and a light-yellow dress with flowers on it, and had fine features and thin, dark eyebrows. It looked strange seeing a middle-aged woman with a hunting rifle, but Karin had seen it before. Ardan had a white beard and hair framing his lined face. His body was wiry, and, in his eyes, there was a weariness, but also a gentleness. He wore a white and red scarf as well. They seemed like the kind of couple who were the nice older aunt and uncle of the family, giving too many sweet biscuits to visitors and spoiling the young kids. But now, they looked traumatized. Still, they had stayed, and Karin respected this. Members of the families that stayed had all been required to take up a weapon to keep their families safe. Karin felt pride in the courage of her people right now. They wished the couple well, and to stay safe, and they moved on. As they walked through the buildings, Karin turned to Sarah.

"I'm going to take you to Aram's bakery."

"There's still a bakery here?" Sarah said. She sounded surprised.

"Yes, it still operates and provides us bread."

As they moved towards the building, the savory, familiar smell of dough baking—a warm, welcoming scent, almost sour and sweet mixed together—surrounded them. They saw the gaping stone structure of an oven with a dark passageway into its heat, the flames inside, glowing red. A man in an apron, grey pants, and a white shirt appeared. He had flour on his face, arms, legs, and in his hair. He smiled widely.

"Kari," he said. They embraced.

Karin introduced Sarah and Marcel to Aram.

"Pleased to meet you," he said nodding to both of them.

Sarah hesitated to offer her hand and then did with uncertainty. He took her hand awkwardly and shook it, looking down. Karin chuckled to herself.

"Would you like some bread?" he asked, turning back to his oven and pulling out a large metal tray of flatbread.

"Yes, *zor spas*, thank you." Sarah laughed at her little mistake of repeating the same word in Kurdish and English. Aram ushered them into his lounge room and pointed to the cushions on the floor. Sarah and Marcel followed and sat down near the wall. Karin stayed next to Aram and offered to help him, while Roza went and spoke to Aram's wife, Araz. Aram brought out a plate of his bread with some olive oil, and olives in a small patterned bowl. He placed this down on the rug in front of them. Araz followed with a pot of tea on a tray, and Roza carried the six small porcelain cups. Karin came in as well. They all sat on the rug together.

"Do you mind if I ask, Aram, why you stayed here when the conflict started?"

"How could I leave? Some of us could not leave our homeland. I'd rather die here, than surrender our land. My role is to keep these soldiers alive while they fight." He looked down at the plate of mostly eaten bread and olives and did not raise his eyes.

"That's very admirable, Aram," Sarah said.

Karin nodded. "We could not go on without you and your family."

"Of course, Kar. We are here for you."

"Thank you, Aram," Karin said. She stood up and walked into the kitchen. After some chatting, Karin signaled to Roza and the others that they needed to leave.

"Thank you for your hospitality," Sarah said.

"No problem, Sarah. *Zor spas* for reporting on what's happening," he said.

"Of course. I hope you stay safe."

"May *Xwa* be with you as well."

"*Zor spas*," Sarah nodded and smiled.

As they entered the next building, Sarah asked Karin, "Did many people stay in Kobane?"

"Yes, some. There are some families in Kobane. As you know, Roza's family stayed, and so did mine. We have pushed Daesh back so far that we have seventy percent of the town now. We will push them right out soon. Some of the families have little children, and they still have a school class here."

"The main reason Karin and I joined the YPJ was to defend the people who remained here," Roza said from the back of the group—this was the first thing she had said in a long time. Karin noticed she didn't say much around Sarah. Understandably though, given what they been through this week.

"Really? So, there are little children here?" Sarah asked.

Karin nodded.

"Forgive me for asking this, but why did they stay?"

Karin paused, feeling a vast distance between herself and this woman that spanned oceans.

"I think it is difficult for others to understand, those who are not from this land, those who are not Kurds."

"Yes, but I want to understand," Sarah answered.

"We have fought for this land for many decades now, and we only won Kobane back for our people in 2012. Our land is our identity, our connection to our culture, families, ourselves. So, for us, our question is not how could we stay? Our question is how could we leave?" Karin looked into Sarah's face to see if she understood, and then looked at Roza who was nodding.

Karin touched her weapon that hung around her neck. In this moment, she wished she was on the frontline. Firing at the enemy was simpler than this. She felt exposed and self-conscious; her cheeks were heating up.

"I understand," Sarah said. "I admire that. My family moved around a lot when I was a child. I don't have a connection to a particular place. I can see your connection, and, in a way, I envy it."

Karin didn't know what to say, so she said nothing. Marcel continued to film, and Karin hoped that she hadn't gone bright red on camera. Then again, did it really matter? He began to film the room in which they had paused, and then they moved towards the opening. This part of the trip was going to be more dangerous, and Karin was reluctant to take Sarah and Marcel into this. Anything could happen. Karin explained to Sarah and Marcel that soon they needed to run across the street and above them were known snipers. She explained she could not guarantee their safety.

"Do you still want to see the hospital?" Karin asked Sarah.

"Definitely. I came here knowing the danger. It's part of my job. Not saying I'm not scared, though."

"Okay. Stay close to us, and run fast, keep your head down and your body low; it makes it harder for them."

"Okay." Sarah turned to Marcel. "We will stay down and low, won't we?"

"Yes, Sarah, of course." He nodded at Karin. Marcel did not speak much, but Karin could see that between these two, there was a silent connection of complete understanding. There was an element of familiarity like an old married couple between them— she heard it in the tone of voice in which he answered Sarah, which reflected a cheekiness and an ease.

"Excellent. Roza, can you come here for a minute?"

Karin pulled Roza aside.

"You'll need to protect them from the rear, but of course the most important thing is to just get across quickly."

"Yes, Karin," Roza answered with an impatient inflection in her voice.

"Okay, sorry. Of course, you know."

Karin patted her on the back, briefly and strongly, and motioned for them to get ready to leave the door onto the street. The afternoon sun shone, white like desert sand in her eyes. Karin stood at the doorway and paused. With her hand, she motioned for them to stop, then signaled for them to come with her quickly. She looked around and above them but knew that was futile—you wouldn't see your killer. Karin ducked her body right down and bent her knees; almost like a human paperclip, she lowered her head as well. She started to run and felt the presence of Sarah right behind her, down low and running. Suddenly, the sound of gunfire all around them shattered the still, sun-lit morning. Bullets roared, pelting the dust and exploding walls on the other side of the street. Dust rose around them as they continued to run. Karin looked back at Sarah, who looked straight ahead, determined.

As objects were being blown into the air around them, the four of them sprinted. Karin heard Roza fire a few times at the back. Finally, they reached the other side of the street and ran into a severely damaged building, ravaged by war—a haven for Karin and the others. They threw themselves down onto the floor and Marcel ran into the wall, only stopping himself with his hands.

Karin was breathless and turned to see the others, who were also recovering. She asked Sarah, Roza, and Marcel if they were okay.

"I'm okay," Sarah answered, breathing heavily, buckled over with her hands on her knees. Roza nodded, and Marcel looked back at Karin as he leaned on the wall. After some moments, catching their breath, Karin asked Sarah if she wanted to go in. Sarah nodded at Karin, looking surprisingly composed for someone who had just been shot at.

They make them strong in that country of hers. Karin patted Sarah's arm.

"You sure?"

"Yes, thanks. I've been in war zones before, but it never seems to get any easier," Sarah chuckled, breathlessly.

"I guess not." *But, it's different when it is your people, your land and your loved ones being blown up or killed.*

"Can I ask you a question?" Karin turned to Sarah.

"Of course."

"Why do you put your life in danger in these situations?"

"A lot of people ask me that." Sarah paused and touched her watch.

"My best friend gave me this watch for my birthday. He always said to me, 'Take life by the balls and live every moment, do something of significance for others.' When he died in a motorbike accident, I requested an assignment with the Foreign Affairs bureau.

"I had always wanted to give a voice to people who didn't have one and to tell their stories. I was already working for the ABC, but now I knew what I needed to do. Since then, I've been all around the world, and covered conflicts, famines, civil wars… To be honest, I was recently going to quit. It can be draining, seeing the worst of the world all the time. I'm glad I didn't, though, now that I get to cover this story." She smiled at Karin; a melancholy expression had rested on her features. Her eyes looked down at her watch as she touched its leather.

"Thanks for telling me that," Karin said. "I'm very sorry for your loss. I appreciate what you're doing. You're a brave woman."

Sarah looked surprised. "Thanks, Karin, but you're the brave ones."

She signaled to Karin and Roza. Marcel came over to them, setting up his camera. A woman with a scarf around her head and dark hair pulled into a messy bun greeted them with a wide, white grin. Karin embraced her and then turned to them.

"This is Evin. She's a doctor here who stayed to help us on the frontline."

"Pleased to meet you."

Evin put her hand out to Sarah, which surprised Sarah, but she accepted the outstretched hand. Karin knew most of the time it lifted the spirits of her friends to meet journalists from around the world. Karin had spent many hours at Evin's house when she was studying, asking questions about medical conditions or diseases; she had also observed her working at the hospital. Karin felt an ache, a longing for the resumption of her study; for a life that seemed so distant now.

"Can I ask you some questions?" Sarah asked Evin.

"Of course."

She led Sarah further into the makeshift hospital where people lay on beds, with rudimentary equipment they had salvaged from the Kobane hospital which had been bombed by Daesh. It was completely destroyed. Here, people had bandages on their heads or arms, and were lying in beds in rows. Nurses attended to them as best they could with equipment that was rudimentary and basic. They obtained any medical supplies they could, bandages and gauzing, from abandoned chemists. They treated the wounded coming in, but they also had to send patients either to other parts of Syria, which was dangerous, or over the border to Turkey, which was an unsafe journey. Karin decided to let them go in together. She knew that Evin had very good English and would be informative for Sarah. Karin and Roza both leaned on the wall and sat down on the ground.

"Roza, *chawa ye?* You've been very quiet."

"Yeah. I'm okay, Kar. Feeling a bit better now," Roza answered.

"After we've finished this with Sarah and Marcel, I want to talk to the Commander about rescuing Ashti. We need to plan."

"Yes, I've been thinking that too. We have to act straight away. We can't allow them to suffer anymore or to be moved somewhere else."

"I agree. I promised Sozan the day she died we would get them out. We will save them."

"We will, Kar." Roza put her arm around Karin. Karin put her head on Roza's shoulder, and they sat in the luxurious silence of years of closeness.

- 20 -

Roza

Roza looked at Karin keeping watch near the window of the building behind a dirty curtain. Karin moved over and sat on the floor next to her, leaning on the wall. She settled in and closed her eyes to rest for a bit.

She always was protective, Roza thought, remembering when she was in primary school one morning and was late to school. Roza's hair was knotted and stringy—she had not brushed it properly. Her mother left for work early, and Roza had slept in. She had dashed off to school and plonked herself down on the mat; all the other kids were staring at her, their eyes wide, burning fire into her cheeks. Adrenalin pulsed through Roza, but Karin had smiled at her, and Roza sat next to her. Khamed, the largest boy in the class, who was always laughing loudly at the other kids in the midst of lessons, smirked and sniggered behind Roza's back. All at once, she felt a yank, pulling her jumper straight backward, and it began to tighten around her neck; she gasped and fell back. She was struggling for air as the neckline pushed into her throat, and it felt like it would choke her. Her voice was muted, her throat tight. Karin had launched herself onto Khamed and pushed him backward. Roza was released; she grabbed her neck and gulped for air. Khamed, breathless and humiliated, tried to conceal this with a cocky laugh as he sat up again. Karin moved back.

"Don't ever do that again," she said, pointing at him. The teacher came in and yanked both of the girls outside—she shouted at them and gave them a lunchtime detention and ten strikes from the wooden ruler on the hand. This was the way of their childhood. She touched the AK47 sitting on the bench next to her. These guns represented freedom, she thought. Things have definitely changed, and they will never return. She felt grateful to Allah that her father was supportive of women's rights and wasn't brutal like others were. But it was her mother, Naze, who had introduced her to the writings of Abdullah Ocalan—Apo as they called him, 'Uncle'—with his beliefs in seeking equality for women and a democratic socialist state for the Kurdish people.

Roza's mother had been raised by a violent, alcoholic man, and she had chosen Roza's father, Bazan, as he was opposite to her own. Bazan was quiet and somewhat distant, but benevolent. He spent hours in his shed, making and fixing things; he was a mechanic by trade. Naze had started to read 'Apo' on her breaks at the shop. She became committed to his ideals and read his many books, obtaining them from the library. Naze read them to Roza, and now Roza could not believe his vision was so close to becoming a reality. Already a Kurdish region in Iraq existed, and more autonomy was the goal. It seemed that now was the best possible chance of it finally happening. As in the agony of childbirth, through the most horrendous circumstances of suffering, Roza prayed that possibly now Apo's visions might be birthed. Karin stirred in her position sleeping against the interior wall. She started to wake up at the same time that Sarah and Marcel came out of the hospital.

"Well, that was confronting…but so amazing what they have done with so little."

"Yes, I know, isn't it?" Roza said to Sarah.

The four of them moved through the buildings to return across the street again, crouching low and running through the deafening gunfire. This time though, Marcel and Sarah seemed a bit more confident. When they had walked through a few buildings again, Sarah stopped Karin to ask her some more questions.

"Tanah told me some things about your training when you came into the YPJ. I wanted to ask you, specifically, about what she mentioned."

"Of course," Karin said.

"She told me that when you undergo training, you need to renounce marriage and children and all of that world. Is this true?"

"Yes, it is," Roza answered. "When we enter the training, our Commander tells us: from now on, you are not part of society. You renounce all of it; you exist outside of it, and you need to put it out of your mind."

"So how did you feel about that, having Yezdanser?" Sarah asked Roza.

"I'm fighting for him, so of course I cannot forget him. I cried every night for ten nights when we got to the training camp. It felt as if a part of me had been blown off in battle. Then one morning, I woke up and felt numb. I didn't cry anymore. It was as if something had died inside me, like I had been mourning the loss of my own life with Yez and now—somehow, I had let go."

Roza was surprised by how much she had revealed to Sarah. It made her feel vulnerable. She was relieved when Karin stepped in and answered, "Most of us who were single when we enlisted agreed to this creed that we would never return to domestic life—that was not our life anymore. I did this. I will not leave the army; a free Kurdistan is what I want. This is my life now. This is what I choose."

"So, you're not disappointed that you will not have a partner? Or children?"

"No," Karin said, looking straight at Sarah. "What is the point of having these if we are not free? Also, what choice does a woman have here? She can become subservient, or she can be liberated by fighting. In this uniform, with this gun, everyone has respect for us, including men. If we do not have this gun, maybe it will go back to before. Being in the army is liberation for us; why would we want anything different?"

"Right," Sarah said, and with a mischievous look in her eye, added, "so there is no flirtation between you and any of the men, Karin?"

Roza laughed, and shot Karin a knowing look.

"Of course, not," Karin answered unconvincingly, laughing.

"Let's go back," Roza suggested, still smiling.

They all turned and began the walk back through the buildings; this was going to be a big day, with massive plans to execute. Roza glanced over at Karin walking ahead. She always walked with such straight, confident strides, with purpose, as if she was leading people, even if no one was following. In some ways, Karin was always leading someone. Mani had always followed her. Karin could be bossy at times, Roza chuckled to herself, but she knew it was out of concern.

Thank goodness, Sarah and Marcel are leaving so on, we can focus on getting Ashti and the girls safe. Roza liked Sarah, but was beginning to feel impatient. She was tired of feeling self-conscious as well, like her whole world was under examination, under a microscopic gaze that could almost burn up her existence, like a leaf under a cruel boy's magnifying glass.

Once they reached the compound, they said their goodbyes to Sarah and Marcel. Sarah would now spend two days with Nasrin and Farhan, and film with him.

"Send our regards to them. Tell them we will talk to them soon," Roza said to Sarah, throwing Karin a cheeky look.

"Ah, of course I will. I imagine you would be very close with them." Sarah seemed to be picking up the subtext Roza was hinting at, though she seemed not to want to pry.

"Yes, we are." Roza still looked sideways at Karin, who was looking straight at Sarah and ignoring Roza's teasing.

"We're good friends," Karin said, finally entering the conversation.

"Okay, excellent, I will tell them you will talk to them soon." Sarah looked amused and curious, but she seemed to be suppressing it. "*Zor spas,* girls. I've learned so much from you. I'm so grateful to have had this time with you. You're truly amazing. I wish you continued safety and success. I'll be coming back to see you again—hopefully, after complete victory. I will be back, regardless."

"Thank you, Sarah, for your coverage of this war and for telling our story. I look forward to seeing you again," Karin said.

"*Zor spas*," Roza said, smiling at Sarah, finally feeling warm towards her. Roza was relieved that the examination was over.

***

Half an hour later, Roza, Karin, Tanah, and Beritan were discussing the mission to save Ashti and the three other girls. The Commander explained how one of the girls had managed to keep her phone and contacted the YPJ. It had taken her a while to able to ring when her captors weren't present. The YPJ then contacted Commander Beritan saying they had found Ashti. Karin grabbed Roza's hand. Roza squeezed it.

"Of course, she's so scared. They've been raped and tortured, and she thinks they may be sold again at the market. She's terrified of being sent to someone worse. One of the girls is ten years old, and she has been raped multiple times by the three men in the house," continued the Commander.

Roza looked down at her hand in Karin's. She found it so hard to listen to this, what these animals were doing. She had seen the footage of Daesh men boasting about buying Yazidi girls for the price of two loaves of bread, as if they were animals; it made her physically ill. Roza had watched it with Nasrin on one of her visits. The three women sat engrossed in what the Commander was saying, absorbing every detail. Roza knew that anything missed or neglected could mean the death of one of the girls, or one of them.

Torani's death played on Roza's mind. What if something like that happened again? What if Karin was killed? Roza wouldn't be able to cope. *What if I'm killed, what about Yez*? But then, what choice did they have? They had to press on and do what they had promised Sozan. Commander Beritan explained that one man would be left on guard when the other men went out. Roza and her unit had a forty-minute window to save the girls. The Commander gave the women a sketch of the building and the layout of the room the girls were in, and a map of the best way to access it. They all stood up. The Commander gave Roza a formidable hug and kissed her three times.

"May *Xwa* keep you safe. Bring these women back to us."

She embraced Karin and then Tanah as well. Roza and Karin took the map away and planned out their attack. Roza felt her pulse quickening as they got their weapons ready and clipped their magazines into the drum. None of them spoke. There was a palpable, unifying feeling between them. They each had a knife strapped to them; they had handguns and their AK47s as well. Roza looked at Karin. They did not speak, but both knew what the other was thinking.

* * *

Roza, Karin, and Tanah moved through the buildings with internal holes, crouching down, not stopping to talk to any of the soldiers or families along the way. There was only a narrow window of time in which they could succeed, and they were not going to jeopardize this mission. When they executed missions, Roza felt like she was in a trance, focusing only on the different steps and processes of the task that they were doing. She had to still her mind and her spirit and walk quietly inside. There was a somber, serious feeling between them. Roza's body became mechanical; all three of them moved quickly, knowing every moment was crucial.

Finally, they reached the edge of the Kurdish territory. The street was deserted, dusty, quiet, and eerily still. There was no movement outside as they gazed out of a gap in the dirty window-pane. One small bird flew down into the gutter of the desolate street. There was a sand-colored building directly opposite them, with a shop on the corner. The building was two stories, and had a staircase climbing the side of it. This was it. The corner store was abandoned; its windows were smashed in. Karin pointed to the shop and nodded. This was the place.

"Okay, it's time. Follow me. May *Xwa* protect us all," Karin said.

Roza looked at her and nodded. Adrenalin pulsed through her; she knew there could have been anyone watching. She stayed close behind Karin. They crouched down and ran across the street, making it safely to the side of the shop. As they got closer, Roza noticed the black spray-painted Daesh symbols, 'Owned by ISIS,' menacing and large on the walls. They crouched down and moved swiftly down the alleyway.

Roza held her handgun ready; Karin and Tanah had their weapons in front of them. They caught sight of the building where the girls were being kept. There was a window above the back door of the building, and a chair beside it. They saw a man sitting outside, his clothes as black as a raven, with a black bandana on his head. He was looking at a magazine and laughing; a machine-gun sat on his lap.

Roza's throat tightened. They paused. Roza touched Karin on the back and motioned for them to get closer. They moved quietly, step by step, edging closer to him. Roza stared at his face, looking for any sign that he had heard them, when all of a sudden, he looked straight at her. Karin already had her weapon pointed firmly at his head, and fired one precise shot.

It went straight through his forehead, forming a small red blood mark. His head slumped down instantly, and his body fell forward. His skull had been torn open at the back, and blood and brains oozed out. Karin pulled Roza onward, and Tanah followed. They ran towards the building. Roza pushed Tanah and Karin back, and shot her handgun at the door behind the dead Daesh man. Plaster, wood pieces, and dust filled the air around them. Time was limited now; they had to rush. Roza led them inside, down a small corridor, to a room down the end of the hall. They could hear women's voices, muffled but frantic.

"We're here girls, don't be scared. Can you move the chairs from the door?" Roza said, into the door. They could hear commotion and scraping of the floor; every moment now was crucial. It seemed like an eternity as Roza waited again for them to say it was clear.

"Clear?" she called through the door.

"Yes," a familiar voice said.

Roza shot again through the door handle and lock, and kicked it open. She saw a small girl in the corner who had a black eye, tied up to a chair. Another teenage girl was tied up next to her, and was moving in her chair, agitated. A woman who appeared to be

214

around twenty years old, looked at them with fear and relief, breathing heavily and trying to speak through the gag.

Then Roza saw Ashti. Her face was blotchy and bruised, her beautiful features swollen from being struck. Roza ran to her and began cutting the ropes, releasing the gag from her mouth. She grabbed her and held her. Karin and Tanah released the other girls. Roza signaled to be quiet, her hand on her mouth, and motioned for them to follow.

Out the back door, they ran past the dead man. The girls held hands pulling each other through. One gasped, and the ten-year-old was crying quietly as they saw his dead eyes and his obliterated head. They moved down the narrow lane and then reached the end of the shop. Roza peered around the corner and looked down the street; it was empty. She couldn't believe it. Turning to Karin, Roza nodded. She led the unit towards the street to run across to safety. She was the first to move out onto the street, and the others followed. Four of them were in the middle of the road when they saw two figures of black, moving. Then shots began to fire, shattering the dirt around them.

Roza fired back, as did Karin. They could see several men advancing towards them.

"*Run!*" Roza screamed.

She stopped and fired her AK47. Karin had also stopped, and began to fire as well. The girls ran past them, screaming. Tanah hurriedly ushered them inside the building. Three Daesh men fell onto the street dead, and Roza felt something slam into her arm. Wetness and shock filled her. Karin supported Roza across the street towards the door and into the passageway. Roza was bleeding from a deep wound in her arm, but there was no time to stop.

Roza and Karin yelled at the girls to keep running. The women sprinted and ducked between the gaps in the buildings, squeezing through spaces and moving through the holes, for what might have been twenty minutes. Roza held her arm as she ran and kept checking that Ashti was in front of her. Once they reached the house of Karin's family friend, Behrain, they finally stopped running. Everyone was crying. The house was empty, and the girls embraced each other in the small lounge room. Roza fell onto Ashti, weeping bitterly. She couldn't stop thinking of Sozan, and her chest was tight with pain.

Ashti whispered in Roza's ear, "Thank you, blessed sister." Karin walked over to them both and embraced them, as they all collapsed down onto the cushions. Ashti didn't know Sozan was dead, and Roza was certainly not going to tell her right now.

- 21 -

Karin

Ashti was taller than Sozan, with long, thin limbs and clavicle bones that protruded out of her chest in a defined manner. She had always seemed to Karin like a tall sea-bird, fine and delicate. Sozan was strong and wiry in comparison. Ashti's hair was darker than Sozan's, and she had brown eyes that seemed to be permanently inquisitive. She sat in the corner of the lounge room with cushions around her lower back, drinking a cup of tea, and blowing on it to cool it down. Karin walked over and sat next to her. She noticed the black bruising on her wrists and arms.

"Hi, Kari. Is Roza's arm okay now?"

"Yes, it's bandaged up. Thankfully, it was shrapnel, so there were only superficial wounds. It should heal quickly."

"Zor spas, Karin, for saving us."

"Of course, Ashti. We couldn't leave you there. I promised your sister; she was so determined that she would free you. And she would have."

"Yes, she would have," Ashti said. She offered a weak smile.

"She loved you so much."

"I loved her more than anything."

Ashti had tears in her eyes.

"This was found in her possessions," Karin said. She handed Ashti a crumpled picture of Sozan, taken with Ashti and her mother and father years before. Its edges were jagged and worn.

"She was never without this."

"Thank you so much." Ashti took it. Looking at Sozan's face, she kissed it and held it close to her chest. Tears rolled down her cheeks.

"Your sister was a true martyr, brave and strong. All of us are devastated, particularly Roza and me. You know how close we were. We miss her so much."

Ashti nodded to Karin. Karin put her arm around her. Ashti flinched.

"Sorry, my shoulders have bruises on them from the beatings."

Karin could see the tears in Ashti's eyes, and her apprehension at being touched. Pulling away a little, she said, "Sorry, I had no idea. You poor thing. I'm so sorry."

"Thanks, Karin." Ashti looked down; she seemed to be becoming overwhelmed. Her cheeks were blotchy red, and she looked down onto her lap. Karin's eyes filled with tears, and somehow, she felt Sozan's presence with them, and her satisfaction that her sister was safe. But she knew Sozan would be devastated to see the pain her sister had gone through. Karin saw in Ashti's eyes elements of Sozan's strength. She lit up a cigarette and offered Ashti one. She said no. Karin wanted to stay with her for a long time, but Ashti had to leave for Suruc, where the refugee camp was waiting. They stood up and embraced, Karin careful not to touch her shoulders.

"I hope you can recover, inside and outside, quickly. May *Xwa* keep you safe. We may visit you soon."

"Thank you so much, Karin. I can't express in words my gratitude for what you have done." Ashti began to get emotional, her eyes were already pink and swollen from crying. "I would have died if I had to stay there any longer. I may have done something to myself if I had not been rescued by you. Now, I have to live without my sister, which is unbearable. My anger for these men eats me up inside."

"And for me, as well."

"Yes. We can't give in to them, can we?"

"No, we can't let them win this. We'll regain our lives eventually, even though nothing will be the same 'cause Soz is gone. But you're alive, thank God. She would want you to embrace your life and honor her."

"Definitely. I will honor and love Soz till the day I die. She was always stronger than me. She fought Dad and defended me many times against his violence. She would take a beating instead of me until she couldn't take anymore. Eventually, her strength meant she had to go. She did ask me to leave with her, but I was too weak. My life was never the same without her. We had only just reconnected in the last few years. I guess I can be thankful that we had that time."

"I can tell you that Soz always talked about you," said Karin. "She watched your life from a distance. She always told us with pride what you were doing, when you were studying teaching at university. She told me how happy she was that you had become close again."

"Thank you for telling me that Karin. I appreciate that."

"It's true. Sozan was an amazing warrior; but mostly, she was my friend." Karin's voice began to break up. "She was a true friend, who gave her life for us. I'll never be able to thank her, and I'll never know anyone like her again."

Karin looked away. She didn't like to get emotional at the best of times, and especially now when Ashti was going through so much pain. Ashti touched Karin's arm.

"Yes, she was."

Ashti couldn't speak after this and had begun to cry. Karin gently hugged her.

"You're strong like Sozan. I can see her in you. She would be so happy you're free. That's all she wanted," whispered Karin.

"I have to go," said Ashti, wiping her eyes. "They want me to go outside and wait for the transport. May *Xwa* be with you, and bring you safely back to us."

"Thanks, and with you as well. We will see you soon."

Ashti walked slowly, as if in a dream, into the other room to gather her things. Karin watched her leave, feeling as if Sozan had died in front of her again. She felt a longing she could not express, for life as it was before this deathly chaos.

***

The following day Karin found herself in a trance as she loaded seventy-five bullets into the magazine of her weapon. She was sitting on the veranda. The seat was dusty and the day was warm for this time of year, the sun bitingly strong, which was why Karin was sheltering under the eave.

"Are you okay?" Roza asked.

"Yeah, I'm alright." Karin faced her.

"I can tell you're not."

"It's just Ashti and Sozan," Karin said. "I thought I would feel relieved or something when we saved Ashti and the girls. I'm glad about that, but I still have this ache in the back of my throat. I can't swallow properly. I can't explain it."

"I feel the same." Roza leaned down and hugged Karin from the side.

"At least we have each other."

"Yes, always. Maybe we should go to see our families? Daesh is almost out of Kobane, and we are close to victory. Maybe now is time for me to see Yez. What do you think?"

"Yes, I think that's a good idea," Karin answered. "The Commander suggested we should."

"The thing I'm worried about," said Roza slowly, "is that if I see him, I may not be able to leave him again."

Karin stood up and looked into Roza's face.

"Maybe you should think about staying with him, Rozi."

Roza didn't speak straight away; she looked at Karin with a furrowing brow. Then she softened.

"I want to Kar, of course I do. But then I think of everyone who has died for us and for Kobane. How can I dishonor them and leave?"

"The battle is largely won now. I think you should consider it, Rozi. Yez needs you too. I wouldn't want anything to happen to you. I couldn't bear it."

"I know he does," she said. "For the first time since joining, I have seriously thought about leaving, especially after Sozan's death. I'm feeling like I can't stay here anymore. I think you're right, Kar."

"That's great, Rozi. Yez will be very happy to have you back."

"I think I have done Ser proud now. Hopefully, anyway, I can go back to Yez and be with him. It's all I want now."

"Of course, Ser would be proud of you. He always was, anyway."

"Thanks, Kar. Let's get something to eat. I can smell something good." Roza embraced Karin and took her under her arm. They went into the lounge room where they were met with the sweet, savory aroma of dolma, white goats' cheese, and flatbreads, with three teapots placed in between the food. The girls sat on the floor on their cushions. Karin smiled at Tanah and sat next to her.

***

After lunch, Karin went up onto the roof; she had not been up there for a long time. She lit a cigarette and looked across Kobane, feeling satisfied that she had been a part of driving Daesh from their place. She looked across to the outskirts of the city, beyond the hills to the edges of the desert that surrounded Kobane. She had always loved the desert colors, the off-white and rich cream colors of this place. Mountainous crevices stood silently above, with centuries of history carved through them. The ancient whisperings of people long past seemed to sing to her about the richness of her land and her ancestors' presence. Where was *Xwa* amidst all of this pain? *Why can't you end this*? She prayed to him now.

Karin remembered one day coming home from school and seeing her father, sitting reading the newspaper, with his pipe resting precariously on the side of his mouth. She approached him and asked if women could be educated and have careers, because the teacher had said that not everyone believed women should, according to Islam. Her father had looked at her and slapped his legs, signaling for Karin to sit on his lap. She climbed up.

"Some people interpret the Quran this way, Kari."

"Yes, but what do you think, Dada?"

He looked at her closely and seemed to be choosing his words.

"I think women, especially you, have been made by *Xwa* with talents. I don't see why he would do this if you were meant to hide them. I'm not a scholar of the Quran, and I'm not really religious, as you know. I don't pretend to know *Xwa*'s will. I have always taken a simple approach. To me, I feel you of all people should use your talents. Don't waste them. I don't know books, but I do know the soil—olives as they ripen, the scent of the leaves early in the morning, the smell of the soil after the rain. This is the God I know."

Karin's grandfather had been a Zoroastrian. He used to say it was the original religion for Kurds, and argue good-naturedly with her grandmother, who was Islamic. He would say something controversial to get a reaction from her grandmother, and then look at Karin and wink. She would react, but then end up laughing and sometimes, her grandfather would pull her over to him and onto his lap. His teasing always ended with her grandmother rolling her eyes and chuckling.

Karin could see why Aster was sometimes ambiguous about aspects of Islam. Sometimes her father chose to pray, 'prayers from his ancestor's religion' as he would say. When Karin's mother was not around, he would often tell her that Zoroastrianism was much simpler and to him, it was pure. He talked about the similarities between the two religions, though, and preferred to believe in a union of belief. As Karin's mother was Islamic, he observed Ramadan and other religious customs. Now, being in this war, Karin wondered—what did she believe? At this moment, she could not decide. She simply prayed to the

God of the desert, as she called him. If she survived this war, then maybe she would think about it. Roza touched Karin on the back, and she jumped. Roza had followed her up to the roof. Karin smiled and offered her a cigarette. Roza took one and lit up as they stood looking at Kobane.

"Have you ever questioned our religion?" Karin asked. Roza paused. She had not expected this question.

"Occasionally," she said. "Especially now. If there is a God, I hope He sees us. He sees what we do, our sacrifice and welcomes us in death. I feel as if He's loving. I don't know why; it's just a feeling inside, despite everything." She looked down.

"I know what you mean, Rozi. I'm not as sure as you, but I hope you're right." Karin and Roza looked into the streets of Kobane below; they could see explosions in the distance. The war never stopped. The YPG's shots flashed bright red across the sky in the distance, and they could hear the sound of the artillery. In some strange way, they felt as if they existed in a sanctuary above it, even if only for these small moments.

***

Two days later, Karin and Roza were traveling back from combat in an area about ten kilometers away from the compound. They were both more exhausted than usual. Karin felt she was becoming tired easily these days. The sun was setting over the hills in the distance, with vibrant pinks, orange, and grey-blues painted across the sky. Reynaz was driving them back to the base. They sat on the back of the truck; their guns slung over their shoulders; as this part of Kobane was relatively safe. Karin took Tanah's sunglasses from her lap and was putting them on, laughing, and making funny poses. Roza and Tanah were laughing at her. Karin fell sideways as the car hit a hole in the road, and then she was pushed back as the car seemed to be accelerating. Karin looked towards Reynaz in the car. Suddenly, Roza was in front of Karin, pushing her backwards as the sound of gunfire assaulted the air around them. Karin only saw Roza's body above and in front of her. The deafening sound of gunshots continued, and Karin felt the impact almost go through her body. She couldn't see—her head was down—and then she felt Roza's body slumped over her.

She heard Tanah screaming. "Roza!" Karin pulled her head up—Roza's body was on top of her. There was something wet on her forearm. Roza's head was forward and limp. Gunfire continued around them. Karin's ears were ringing, and everything seemed to slow down. She felt as if she had left her body and was watching the horrific scene from above. She gently pushed Roza's head up. Her chest and neck were covered in blackened red.

"No! Roza, no!!"

Karin screamed and began to press down on Roza's chest desperately with her sleeve. She pulled off her shirt, and attempted to put pressure on her chest to stop the bleeding. Shots were fired from Jusef in the passenger seat of the car, and Tanah was shooting into buildings from the back as they moved quickly through the streets. Karin heard and saw nothing but Roza's features: the long, black eyelashes, and the small body crumpled before her.

"Stay with me, Rozi," she pleaded, looking into eyes that were only slightly open. "Please stay with me. I can't do this without you. You'll be okay, Rozi..."

Karin pulled Roza closer and rested her head onto her lap. Roza blinked, looking up at Karin.

"You can't die here…for me…"

"Why… not?" Roza managed to utter.

"It's not meant to be like this..." Karin answered, touching Roza's face, weeping uncontrollably. Everything around Karin had narrowed into Roza's face. She only existed here, with Rozi, in this alternate, blurred, blood-filled realm.

Roza gestured for Karin to come close.

"Yez…" she managed to say, breathing out loudly. Her eyes looked upwards, her mouth fell slightly open, and she was gone.

Karin closed her mouth and her dark eyes, and held her close. She rocked backward and forward with Roza in her arms, saying, "Rozi, Rozi… no, not you… Rozi…"

She kissed Roza's cheek. Blood covered Karin's clothes and face, but she didn't notice. Karin saw Roza as a shy, teenager avoiding Sercan's gaze when they first met in the market, and when she laughed at Karin's jokes behind the shed at school. She saw her when she first held Yez in her arms. Flashes of Roza standing above her, taking the gunfire, played over and over in her mind. She laid her face onto Roza's, as the car moved rapidly and roughly through the streets of desolate Kobane. The shooting had now ceased, though Karin hadn't noticed.

- 22 -

Karin

"Karin, can you say something?" Commander Beritan asked, gesturing for Karin to come and stand near the grave.

Karin walked out to the front of the coffin and faced a large number of soldiers, there to honor Roza. She glanced at the crowd of people and saw Nasrin and Farhan. Seeing Farhan was a shock, for some reason. Of course, they would have heard about it, but she didn't expect them to be here. She looked down at the wooden box, feeling completely numb.

"I don't have anything profound to say," Karin said, looking through the crowd of soldiers, straight ahead, trying to maintain her composure.

"How can I sum up what Roza was to me? How can I come close to saying anything worthy of her in a few words? I can't." Her voice disappeared. She looked out over the cemetery and to the many graves with mounds of dirt covering people they had lost.

"She loved Kobane. She loved her son, her husband Sercan, and her family. She loved me…" Karin broke down. "It's too much. She defended me and lost her life. That was Rozi. There's maybe one thing that can sum her up, what she meant to me and to everyone in her life. Her name's meaning, 'Where the Sun Rises.' That is what she was for me—where the sun rose, every morning. She was my sunrise and sunset and everything in between. She was everything to me." Karin could not restrain her tears now.

"Peace be upon her. May *Xwa* keep her now," she managed to say, looking down at the grave and blowing a kiss. She walked quickly back through the crowd of soldiers. Farhan touched her shoulder as she passed, but she was determined to go. She could not be here anymore. It felt as if she was falling into a deep black hole; and if she didn't leave, she would never escape. Making her way back to the car, she returned to the base. She didn't want to stay to hear all of the words that would be said to comfort her, and she didn't want to say something back that she would regret. There was a burning rage within her, and no one could alleviate her pain. If she could have, she would have run at full speed out of that cemetery.

***

Karin looked at herself in the cracked mirror on the wall situated in the lounge room where all the women got dressed. She touched the new lines that she felt had appeared around her eyes. Roza had never put on makeup; she didn't need it. Whenever Roza pulled her hair up into a ponytail, she'd look briefly look into this mirror, before pulling Karin over to it and making a joke about their bed hair.

Karin looked at her own unruly black hair now. She did not want to brush it, or force it to submit. For the first time in this whole three months of fighting, she would not make it submit. She would not brush it. Roza couldn't anymore, so, why should she?

She took the shiny metal silver scissors from the kitchen and grabbed a large, long bunch of hair. It had not been cut for years. Putting the metal jaws around it, she cut straight through it, hearing the sound of metal on metal, and feeling it release a large weight onto the ground. She felt liberated, lighter. Karin continued, and took another chunk of hair and then another; there was no design to it. She felt progressively lighter as each wad of black hair fell heavily onto the ground.

Continuing in an almost frenzied fashion, Karin finally looked into the mirror and saw her hair short around her face, jagged and uneven. Eye-catchingly short. She smiled, feeling completely free. She touched the soft flesh at the back of her neck, felt the gap, and burst into tears, which quickly turned into bellowing laughter.

Rozi would have laughed if she saw this, she would have said, "That's a terrible job, Kari! Now you really will have to wear the headscarf." She wished Roza could say this, and she could hear her deep laughter.

"What have you done?" Tanah said, interrupting Karin's thoughts.

She turned around and smiled tentatively. "Do you like it?"

"Um, well, it needs a little cleaning up." Tanah took the scissors from Karin and started to trim the back of her hair, so it was straight and not uneven. She cut various parts from the back and side, and then she stood back.

"Now, it's better."

"Thanks, Tanah." Karin took one more examining look from all angles, and decided she actually loved it.

"I have to start packing," Karin said, as she made her way into their sleeping quarters.

Tanah followed.

"Where are you going?" she asked, moving towards Karin.

"To Yez."

"Okay, can I help you pack?"

"No, thanks. I don't have much to pack, really." She began shoving clothing into a large, scratchy, khaki rucksack.

"Are you okay?" Tanah asked.

"I am." Karin continued to put her clothes into the bag even more aggressively. "But she's not."

"Stop, Kari." Tanah turned Karin to herself and embraced her.

"It's my fault," Karin said loudly. "You know that, don't you? I'm responsible."

"No, you're not."

"Yes, I am," Karin said, turning back to her clothes, trying to hide her tears. "She wouldn't be in this war if it wasn't for me. I had this dream last night. I was in the kitchen, eating some eggs and drinking tea. I could hear the women laughing and talking in the other room. I felt a wetness on my body and was confused. When I looked in the mirror, I saw blood all over my body, my face, congealed blood in my hair, in sticky blobs. I felt physically sick and started to scream, and then I woke up."

"That's disturbing, Kar. But you're not responsible. Don't flatter yourself. Roza was as determined as we are to fight. No one could've stopped her."

"Maybe that's true… but then she had to go and protect me like that…" Karin wept, and Tanah began to as well.

"She loved you."

"But what about Yez? How will he cope? Will he know his Mama died to save me? I can't bear this… I can't."

Tanah embraced Karin. They stood there for what seemed like a long time, weeping. Finally, Tanah said, "You don't have to go to Yez now if you're not ready. You could wait."

"I have to go now. I can't be anywhere else but with him. We've both lost someone so precious. We need to be together."

"I understand. You're coming back though, aren't you?" Karin turned to Tanah and shook her head to say 'no.' She couldn't utter the word out loud.

"Oh, okay. You always told me you would never leave."

"I know." Karin looked down and took out a cigarette from her packet. She placed it in her mouth and lit up the end, watching the smoke waft away from her.

"I can't leave Yez without any parents. I have to be with him and help raise him, for Roza. She gave her life for me, and I have to honor that. I will be the parent she can't be, now. I will ask her parents if I can live with them."

"I understand," Tanah said. She again embraced Karin and this time squeezed her hard. "May *Xwa* be with you, always."

***

The day was darkening when Karin, Tanah, and the Commander drove across town to the place they had arranged to meet Aster, Maia, Yez, Bazan, and Naze. Karin would convince all of them to leave and go over the border. There was nothing left to do. Karin could not stay any longer. No more lives would be lost between them; she had to protect all of them. With Roza gone, she would insist they leave.

As they drove the forty minutes across town. Karin couldn't believe she was coming back to them like this, without Roz. Tears rolled down her cheeks. She couldn't control it—they kept coming—and she looked out onto the devastated streets as they drove. There was another car with them, which would transport them all to the border. It was a risk. They could be killed crossing, but it was better than staying. Karin didn't want Yez in any more danger. She had used her connections to organize being smuggled across, as the border was still closed. They had found out there were guards that would help them, so she decided she would take her chance. There was no other choice now. She wished so much it was Roza doing this, fulfilling her desire of returning to Yez.

After a little while, they arrived outside the damaged building where their families had gathered to be picked up. She looked down the laneway next to the building, and saw a few small children in the mud, digging, and playing with sticks. She saw a small boy standing with another boy, and her stomach churned. It was Yez. She hadn't seen him for months. Bursting into tears, Karin paused; she didn't want him to see her like this.

After some moments, she walked towards him. He saw her and called out, "Karin, is that you?!"

She had forgotten she had short hair now. Walking over to him, Yez opened his arms to her, and she held him and didn't want to let go. He tucked himself into her body. He was crying now, she felt it, but she couldn't see his face. His little body felt as if it melted into her. She wept as well, and for some moments, they stayed like this.

"Yez... I'm sorry... Your mama was coming back to you... and I'm so sorry..." Karin said to him.

He hugged her tightly, not saying anything. He knew Roza had died; they had told the family the day before. Looking down at his face, she saw Roza and her beautiful face, laughing, playfully hitting Karin with a towel after swimming, riding on the back of the truck making faces. Roza smiling as she rested on her machine

233

gun. His arms wrapped around her middle, Yez looked up at Karin. She saw the look Roza had often given her through her deep, brown eyes, staring up from beneath Yez's brows. Karin knew, at this moment, that she would never leave him again.

Karin had insisted the day before on the phone that they had to leave, and she was not taking no from any of them. She embraced each of them, and told Roza's parents she was sorry. She could barely look in their eyes; guilt made her feel physically sick. But she couldn't focus on her guilt. Getting everyone into the car and over the border was her priority.

They got into the two cars and drove to the area they would walk across to the border. On the drive, Karin, the Commander, and Tanah did not speak. Yez was sitting next to Karin, melded to her body. It was as if he wanted to become part of her. She could tell he was scared. She pulled him close; it was like her heart could not break anymore.

It was silent between them; there was a solemnity about what they were doing. When they arrived, they all got out of the car, and Karin told Tanah she would see her soon. She embraced the Commander. Beritan's eyes regarded Karin for a moment. Karin hugged her, with tears in her eyes; it was hard to be leaving this strong, lovely woman. She noticed Beritan had tears as well, but they both tried to conceal it.

"I will see you in a free Kobane!" the Commander said.

"Yes, you will, my friend. Yes, you will." Karin answered her, smiling as widely she had the day Roza had gotten married and stood beaming next to Sercan.

"May *Xwa* keep you safe. Thank you so much for everything," Karin said to Tanah as she kissed her three times. "I will see you soon."

Walking away with Yez and her family, she looked back and saluted them both. Karin directed the small group towards the path they needed to walk to get to the Turkish border. The border guards she had been in contact would be on duty. There was still danger crossing the border, but Karin didn't care anymore; she had lost all concern when the numbness of grief descended onto her.

They moved through the part of Kobane where Daesh had been pushed back. This way was the only avenue with access to the border. Their small group walked as one organism, as quietly as they could, keeping down low. They passed the ruins of houses that had already been opened up, bare and exposed as, they approached the field where they would cross. The scent of diesel mixed with scorched and burning inanimate objects, as well as the flesh of cows and horses, would never leave Karin.

She checked on her mother, walking with her pack, and her father, then walked over to Roza's parents, putting her hand on her mother's shoulders. Naze looked numb and shell-shocked as if she had seen something unearthly and wrong. She looked straight ahead. *How could she cope with losing Roza?*

Adrenalin coursed through Karin's veins, preparing her in case Daesh discovered them as they walked across the sandy rock-covered expanse between Kobane and Suruc, Turkey. Karin was nervous about how the guards would greet them. She felt as if the loss of Roza and Sozan was happening all over again. It was as if Karin was leaving Roza right now, but she knew Roza was where she wanted to be. She suppressed her emotion for Yez's sake. She felt she was abandoning those they had lost; Sozan, Mani, Sercan, Torani, and even Kobane. But then she looked down at Yez and knew she was doing the right thing. There were police vehicles and army personnel on the Turkish side of the border. But the gate did open to them, and the guards, after looking them over and checking their documents, allowed them through.

On the first night in Turkey, they found sanctuary in a mosque, and stayed there for the following week. They slept in the grounds and on the steps of the mosque. Karin could never fully sleep. Yez slept next to her, curled up close. Roza's family camped next to Karin's, and together they obtained food and water from wherever they could, being given rations of rice, and collecting water from the taps down the road. They had to adjust to being foreigners, with the myriad of different sounds, smells, streets, shops, people; it took time.

After some days and nights in the mosque, Karin checked in what was happening over the border. She often would go to the hill that overlooked Kobane, and could see the bombing and shelling that was destroying her land. Then Karin, Maia, Aster, Yez, and Roza's parents took a taxi to Suruc, where the refugee camps were. Karin's uncle Asgher had gone there months before.

Karin felt like she was in another world driving through streets of shops, tall buildings, apartments and people who made their way around the city, living a normal life. She drank in all the sights: people drinking coffee; smoking pipes on the street; people coming home from work; purchasing fruit and meat; and greeting their families. Life. But Roza should be here. She had fought for this also. Acid rose in the back of Karin's throat.

Following a short drive, they reached the refugee camp, a hastily thrown-together collection of white tents stretching out like an ocean before her. This would be their home until Kobane was freed. Karin hoped this was only a temporary situation and she said a prayer for Roza. At least now her family, including Yez and Roza's parents, was safe.

- 23 -

Karin

May, 2015

Three months of chilled nights and days in the tents of the refugee camp had passed. Now it was time for Karin, Yez, and their families to return to Kobane. A narrow doorway with a wooden wall represented the border between Syria and Turkey, but more importantly, separated them from their place. Karin felt nervous going towards the door. She didn't know how she would feel; after everything she had been through there, would she feel guilty for leaving? Looking down at Yez holding her hand, and seeing how he looked up at her, she knew right then that–she would never regret what she had done.

Sarah and Marcel had told Karin that they would meet her. They were covering the rebuilding of Kobane. Karin was excited to see them, and her joy at the prospect of going home, no matter the devastation, was building up within her now as she queued. Aster was ahead of them, and he turned to her and smiled. Maia was next to him, her small shoulders facing forward, anticipating what they had all longed for.

After thirty minutes of waiting in the queue, it was their turn to go through the gates. Roza's mother Naze and her father, Bazan, were also with Karin; she turned around to make sure they were okay. This would be very difficult for them. They had lost Roza, Sercan, and many other people. As they walked through the doors, Karin saw the familiar sights of the streets she had left. Now, the rebuilding had begun. Karin had seen television news coverage of how Kurds all around the world were celebrating this victory. She felt elated at how the Kurds banded together to achieve this, and how they had unified to defeat Daesh. Karin had never felt so proud to be Kurdish.

Yez gasped next to her, surveying the streets and demolished buildings. He tightened his grip on her hand and seemed to be holding his breath. Did he feel like he would see Roza around the corner? Did he see her face in every shop? Was he remembering the trauma of being here while the war raged on the other side of town? This was where they would walk to get fruit, or ice creams together.

Shards of bricks lay on top of each other, wired metal formed naughts and crosses in the sky from the large concrete slabs that had been torn open. Buildings were blown apart; white and tan dirt mingled together; cars that had been on fire were now simply orange, red, rusted metal frames with rubber wheels torn off. In a few of the buildings, cars had been burnt into metallic shells in their garages, still sitting there as if waiting to be driven. They walked down what had been the main street. There were now people living in Kobane again. Spray painted on the walls was green and red graffiti, as well as people had painted previous house numbers on the ruined buildings so people could find their homes again. Karin looked right towards the main street and down the road to the market where she had spent many mornings shopping. She smiled, noticing the many shops she could see that had opened up. Some of them were rudimentary; she even saw the old ice cream stand down the dusty street. She looked in the other direction and saw the central square of Kobane. Tears formed in her eyes as she saw the eagle that represented their freedom preserved perfectly. She had heard it was the only thing in Kobane that was not destroyed. People had been talking about it as a symbol of their strength and ability to thrive. She noticed that it had been painted green and red in the colors of the YPJ.

Karin and Yez walked across the road to the monument in the middle. Karin saw pictures of the soldiers and friends she had fought with, those who had given their lives for Kobane. She felt proud of her comrades, her sisters, and her small part in the fight for this liberation. Thoughts of Torani, her infectious laughter at the training camp and on the frontline, flashed across her mind. She ached for Torani, who had given her young life, and Sozan and Roza, her precious sisters and friends. The loss of these three women was unbearable. It was a price too high to pay for freedom, but they had willingly paid it.

She moved slowly with Yez around the posters that bore the faces of women and men she knew, and then, they came to her; Roza. She felt her pulse quickening; her stomach felt like it was falling. Her beautiful face, her eyes bright, smiling as she often did before the war. There was a red star above her face with the letters 'YPJ' on it. Yez had already stopped and moved closer to the poster.

"Mama." He touched her cheek in the photograph and kissed it, putting his face close to hers. "Mama…" His bottom lip trembled. Karin stood close, tears in her eyes.

"Yes, your Mama. Look how brave she was."

"Yes." He began to cry. "I wish she was here."

"I know, sweet. She loved you so much. You know she was coming back to you."

"I know," he swallowed, trying to control his emotion. "I wish she had."

"Me too, darling," Karin said, she squatted down next to him and cuddled him.

There was nothing she could say that would change anything. She pulled him close. After some moments, Karin suggested they buy flowers for Roza's grave later on. Yez agreed. Karin heard him breathe in deeply, as if he was trying to be strong. He took Karin's hand. Roza's parents were walking over to the monument, and Karin thought it best if he were not present while they expressed their grief.

Karin and Yez walked back to the other side of the street. Motorbikes had now started to drive around Kobane again, and one beeped them as he went past. The man on the bike smiled at Karin and waved. She waved back—it was Farhan. A jolt of dopamine moved through her whole body, making even her fingertips tingle. Despite everything, she felt an exuberant optimism, seeing that he was well, filled her with joy, and she knew that later she would find where he was living. It was almost hard to comprehend that he had survived when many others hadn't. She felt elation and relief move through her body. Above them, the sky was blue and vast. She looked up. She could not believe she was here; it felt wrong to be here without Roza, but conversely, transcendent. She could barely comprehend the difference between this place and the one where she had been

241

fighting only a few months before. Karin and Yez walked quietly together towards the market. As they approached, she was surprised by the vibrancy and life in the veins of Kobane. Blood was now pulsing through her place again.

Karin saw Ashti in the distance and waved to her. Approaching the fruit shop, she saw an abundance of onions, shallots being delivered by a small car, apples, rich oranges, pomegranates. She smelled the scent of the fruit shop she had loved since a child. She breathed in deeply; it was the fresh bitter scent of oranges mixed with the sweetness of the pomegranates. Such vivid color. Next to the fruit shop, there was a stall of crushed herbs, and vegetables displayed for sale. Next to this, there was a butcher with meat hanging on metal rungs in the street. Whole sections of cows and lambs were dangling on metal hooks, just the way she remembered.

A man in a wheelchair rolled past and nodded to Karin. She noticed there were new pots in concrete boxes on the pavement, housing newly growing plants, bushes, and even small trees. One day, these would provide shade, and be luscious. In the distance, three abandoned Russian tanks faced each, as though they had had an argument and were frozen in some time continuum. They had no wheels, and the burnt metal was a monument to the battles that raged on this very soil. An old man was weeping as he walked down the street. Karin did not know him, but she knew his tears were sorrow mixed with joy to be returning here. She saw motorbikes, small children walking down the street with their mothers, families. Women and men walked with their babies. All were moving around in such a breathtakingly normal fashion. Karin squeezed Yez's hand.

A boy approached, who looked Yez's age. His face lit up.

"Yez!"

"Assan," Yez said, moving closer to the other boy. They hugged quickly.

Both of the boys seemed overwhelmed to see each other, but neither wanted to show it that much. There was an ocean of suffering between them. Now, seeing each other seemed to be like a sighting of land when one is hoping to be rescued from the sea.

"Do you want to play soccer later? I am staying with my grandmother."

"Yes," Yez said. He nodded as Assan moved away, and his mother smiled at Karin.

"Is he your old neighbor?"

"Yes, Aunty. Can I play with him later?"

Karin looked at Yez.

"Of course, sweetheart." She roughed up his hair a little and pulled him close, glad he could resume being a child so quickly. They continued moving along the street. A barber had opened up again, and men sat in their chairs and chatted to other men, their hair wet, receiving haircuts and laughing, their hands flailing about in open expression. The men were getting their beards and hair trimmed as liberally as they wished, another sign of their freedom from Daesh.

Up ahead, Karin saw clothes shops that had opened up again, with jeans, dresses, even costumes for parties in their windows. A toy shop had also re-opened, and Mickey Mouse ears and masks were on display. Balls, chess and checkerboard games, marbles, kites, dolls, and comics spilled out onto the street in a vivid, bold, and defiant cacophony of color. She could not believe the number of people she saw that she knew. She felt exhilarated, despite the devastation; a melancholic joy. She felt guilty for feeling excited, but she was. There was a sinking sensation in her stomach. She could see Roza and Sozan walking down the street like they used to, arm in arm, going to buy some clothes or books or a jacket for Yez.

Karin had lost everyone that meant anything to her, and so had Yez. She couldn't swallow the lump in her throat; it was like when blood falls on the dirt and forms a glob that will not dissipate. Karin paused, stooped down, and picked Yez up into her arms. He wrapped his body around her and buried his head into her neck. She felt a pat on her back and turned quickly to see Aram's kind, lined face smiling back at her. His eyes were teary.

"Karin."

Karin couldn't help it. She embraced him warmly and kissed his cheeks twice, then saw Araz and embraced her as well, holding her tightly.

"You both survived everything? That's so amazing! I'm so glad to see you." Karin felt overwhelmed. She had never found out if they had made it.

"Yes, we were there until the end. It got very, very bad and hard, but thanks to people like you, Kobane was won back. We have opened our shop again, so everyone can come and enjoy our bread in Kobane."

"I'll definitely come and get some bread. I can't wait, can already taste it." She smiled.

Aram looked down at Yez.

"This is Roza's boy, Yez, isn't it?"

"Yes." Karin looked at Yez and pulled him close to herself. "Aram has a bakery. Your Mama loved his bread."

"Oh, good morning, sir," he said.

"Morning, Yez." Aram smiled at Yez, and Karin knew he was thinking of Roza, but she was glad he didn't say anything about her.

"I will come and see you there soon, okay? We have only arrived today."

"Good. I look forward to seeing you."

"Me too, Karin," Araz said, as she touched her on the arm. She and Aram held hands and walked down the street. The sun shone on their backs as Karin watched them walk away. They were late middle-aged, and she felt enormous admiration for what they had risked to stay in Kobane. Karin guided Yez back towards the center square. They saw Roza's parents placing flowers on their daughter's monument. Naze was kneeling before the picture of Roza, and Bazan had his arm on her shoulder. Before they reached them, they saw someone else in the distance—a woman standing in front of a cameraman—Sarah and Marcel. Behind Marcel was a familiar form. But it couldn't be? Was it? Karin's heart began to quicken. As she walked closer, she could tell it was him, Farhan. She would be able to talk to him, but this made her nervous as well.

Seeing the three of them together sent a jolt through all of her nerves; it reminded her of the conflict. Of Roza, Sozan, Torani, of the whole bloody mess, but, mostly of Roza. It wasn't right that she wasn't here. She hadn't talked to Farhan since the funeral. As Yez and Karin walked towards them, she realized that of course Sarah would have contacted Farhan again. She had consulted with all of the journalists in Kobane throughout her coverage and the conflict. Now, he was here.

"Yez, we arranged to meet those people I told you about today. That's them over there. Is that okay?"

Yez nodded. They walked across the road to where the three of them were immersed in their recording. Sarah was speaking to camera. Karin approached cautiously; she felt nervous about seeing Farhan and didn't know what to say. None of them had seen her yet, though, and she was curious to hear what Sarah was saying.

"After six months and two days, the battle with Daesh was won. Now we are three months on from the complete victory of Kobane. Two thousand people stayed after thousands fled over the border. Predominantly, these fighters were women, including the YPJ that came in here to fight Daesh and won. It was the YPJ and YPG Kurdish forces, female and male, that pushed Daesh back 290 kilometers, and also continued to attack other Daesh territories.

"Kobane was the place where the fiercest fighting between Daesh and the Kurds took place. This city represents the first defeat suffered by Daesh, and many see this as a symbol of what could be achieved elsewhere. It is also the place where, for the first time, Kurds from all nations banded together fighting for their people. This had not happened before, and was an amazing demonstration of the bond shared by Kurds.

"This was one of the most dangerous battlegrounds in all of Syria, and now look at it. It's filled with life, vibrancy, markets, children, ice cream shops, barbers, schools. People are even getting married here again. There is a defiant freedom here... A hard-won freedom, through the loss of many people's lives. Before the war, there were 50,000 people in Kobane, and approximately 10,000 people have returned. We will look at how the people of Kobane are rebuilding, and how their victory is a testament to the strength, courage, and fierce spirits that drove out one of the cruelest groups seen in recent times.

"The people of Kobane are rebuilding brick by brick, and reclaiming what Daesh attempted to take but couldn't. Their identity, spirit, and their land. I have met many women and men who gave their lives for Kobane, and I would like to honor them, right now. They were outstanding people who lost their lives but will never be forgotten. There is a memorial here in the town square. Let's look closer."

Sarah motioned for Marcel to stop with the 'cut' symbol across her neck.

"Karin!" Sarah said, opening her arms and motioning her over. She embraced Karin in a strong hug.

"I heard about Roza. I'm so sorry."

"Thank you," Karin said, feeling overwhelmed.

"I'm so glad we could arrange to do this now. Wow, look at Kobane now. I'm blown away. Sorry! Sorry if that sounded bad. It's a saying in my country." Sarah looked mortified at what she had said.

"Don't worry, Sarah, I understand, Karin said, laughing. "Every culture has different sayings." Karin laughed at Sarah's embarrassment and smiled at Marcel, embracing him. She felt she was beyond old traditions now. Farhan moved forward with an unsure gait.

"*Silav,* Karin, how are you? It's been too long. I was so happy to see you earlier…I didn't know if I would see you again," he said, gently.

"*Silav,* Farhan. I know, it has been a few months. I'm good now that I'm back here. Of course, there are memories, about Roz and Soz…" She stopped herself. "It's so good to see you, though." Forgetting her normal traditional, she pulled him into a hug, then felt slightly embarrassed and pulled away again. Karin was so relieved to see him alive. He smiled the widest smile she had ever seen on his face, and seemed a bit flustered, but happy. Karin laughed slightly at herself.

"I never got to say how sorry I was about…" Then he looked
down at Yez. "You know what I mean."

"Yes, thanks, Farhan. You haven't met Yez yet, have you? This is Yez." Karin signaled to Farhan and the others.

248

"This is Farhan—he knew your Mama—and this is Sarah and Marcel. They are all journalists, and they helped us in the battle."

"Hello, Yez, so nice to meet you." Sarah extended her hand to shake his. He didn't fully understand, but took her hand and held it. She moved it up and down and laughed a little at herself.

"Yez is seven years old."

"Nice to meet you finally, Yez."

He looked at her and smiled, and then looked down.

"Have you had a look around? Kobane is regenerating," Farhan said in an excited tone, looking across the street to the new markets. Karin knew that only he could understand how she was feeling right now. He was raised in Kobane; it was in his blood, too.

"We have looked around a bit. It's amazing, unbelievable." She pulled Yez close to herself and hugged him.

"Tanah is here as well," Farhan said. "I saw her earlier."

"Is she? I'm so glad. I did keep in touch, but in the last few weeks I hadn't heard anything. I was worried about her. That makes me so happy—I'll have to find her."

"I can give you her new phone number."

"Thanks so much, I appreciate it."

Farhan smiled at Karin. She felt that familiar nervousness mixed with excitement that she had felt with him before as she smiled back at him, tentative and shy. Their eyes met in an intimacy only they could share, a common knowledge of what the other felt and thought. Of what they had seen, and experienced, in this hellish time. Their shared gaze communicated more than words could utter. Karin surrendered to this feeling now. She didn't want to allow herself to before, but this was her new normal. Life had to go on, and she welcomed it. She did not want to deny her feelings anymore. Wasn't this what she and Roza fought for? Liberty, love, and life. Her eyes looked down, aware that they were ignoring Sarah and Marcel.

"You all must come and meet my family and Roza's," she said. "You have to come and see more of Kobane with us, but first, we will get you some tea."

"We would love to, thank you," Sarah said, as she put her arm on Karin's shoulder. Farhan began to walk next to Sarah. They all walked off towards Roza's parents. Yez held Karin's hand, and Marcel walked next to Yez. Karin looked back towards Roza's monument. She saw Roza wearing her navy-blue shirt and black jeans. Roza looked at Karin, touching the fabric of her purple scarf, she smiled widely, blew a kiss, and then turned and walked away.

- 24 -

Karin

October, 2015

Five months had passed since Karin had walked back into Kobane with Yez, her new and old family. Life in Kobane was bustling and moving again, and presented all of the colors and scents of her childhood. She reveled in the fact that life was being restored somewhat, though they still didn't have electricity all the time. Yez was able to attend the school that started up again in a torn building, with Ashti as his teacher. Before the war, she had graduated, but did not have a position. Karin was so pleased that Roza, Sozan, and Torani's sacrifice had not been for nothing. Her people were rebuilding, and Kobane was breathing again.

Karin still had persistent nightmares though, where horrific images of men, dismembered and bloody, looked at her out of frozen, lifeless eyes. She saw her comrades bleeding, limbs ripped off by mortar fire. She would wake up terrified, with flashes of the explosion that took Sozan away, and Roza's face as she died in her arms. Tonight, she had woken suddenly, and as was her habit, she went outside to look at the sky. Somehow, she felt she could talk to Roza if she looked at the open black glitter-filled expanse above. She felt that Roza would hear her.

Karin was on the veranda that faced the street. It was completely quiet, except for a dog fossicking in rubbish in the alley a few hundred meters away. Kobane was doing well, she thought, considering the widespread destruction of buildings and infrastructure. She lit up her cigarette. Now that she was free from battle and was caring for Yez, she had decided to give up smoking, but smoking was also a reminder of Roza. For now, she continued to do it, knowing that, in the end, it would go.

Standing there gazing into the city that was being rebuilt, but still disheveled and damaged, Karin felt it was like a visual image of herself. Inside, sometimes, she felt fear for no reason: she would experience flashbacks and become tense. If there was banging outside their house, her instant response was to jump up from where she was sitting and move to the window or door and look outside. She wasn't aware of anything around her except this question: was Daesh there again? Yez would ask her; "Is everything okay, Aunty?" and she would suddenly snap out of her fear. When she saw his concerned, furrowed face, she would say, "Of course, love."

Tomorrow, Karin would get Yez ready for school and drop him off. She would go to the hospital, where she was working as a nurse until she could sit her final medical exams and complete training to be a doctor. Yez was enjoying resuming some kind of life, but even he had nightmares where Karin had to comfort him.

"Miss you, Rozi," Karin said to the deaf, cool night air. "So much."

She laughed at herself. It always struck her as strange when she talked to the air. But she couldn't help it.

"I have started to write your story, lovely. Yez will know his mother, everything that I can remember. He will have it written down, and you will never be gone, Roz. Not for me or him."

It was when she had been discussing being back in Kobane without Roza that Amara had suggested Karin write Roza's life. Karin had started with apprehension, but now she was enjoying the process of reliving everything from their childhood and teenage lives. Now she had reached the trauma. This was where she paused.

Karin read in the newspaper about how some people who had suffered trauma were using writing to release their PTSD. She was always skeptical of this kind of therapy, but she had decided to try it; maybe it would help her. The article had said to write about how you felt in a situation and to describe what happened, writing your deepest emotions just for you and not writing for anyone else. She didn't know if it would help, but had started. This she did separately to writing about Roza.

She remembered the first time she wrote anything. She had started with the raw emotion of Mani's death, and by the time she had cried and written a whole page, her pain and anger felt released. She felt exhausted, but strangely lighter, like when she had played soccer and was spent from the effort, but felt her limbs fill with positive endorphins. Her emotions flowed out of her onto the page. She had become addicted to it, and began to write down the trauma and emotion as it came to her. Her biggest desire in life now was to be there for Yez, and to be whole for him. This writing was allowing her to heal. Slowly, she felt, inside, she was clearing out these traumas. Writing Roza's life was also helping.

"Who would've thought, Rozi, that I would be writing? You were the literature-lover, not me. You could've given me tips."

This time Karin whispered, as she did not want anyone from the neighboring dwellings to hear. She blew smoke out into the air and decided to go back to bed. Tomorrow, she would see Farhan as well. Karin smiled, thinking of him.

"You would be proud of me," she whispered. "I have been getting to know Farhan, and now we are together. See, I'm not so set in my ways, Roz. I wish maybe I could've been more expressive at times. I guess we all have our weaknesses. You'd be proud of me, though; I'm more affectionate with Farhan. I'm trying."

Karin laughed at herself. "Night, Rozi." She blew a kiss into the night and went back inside the house. Yez was sleeping soundly in the room opposite; she heard him stirring as she went into her room. Roza's parents slept down the hall. Their house was still damaged from the war; there were holes in the walls, and paint peeling off the interior. They had had to seal up holes made by the YPJ forces in the side walls. There was only a dirt-filled rug on the floor, but it had made it more like home. Gradually, shops were opening, and they could buy blankets and sheets, kitchen items and even decorations.

Yez still had a few of his toys. Karin tried to buy him a few every now and then, when she could afford it. She wanted his life not to be so bare, to not remind him that he had lost a part of himself. But of course, he felt it. Sometimes he was very quiet, and Karin just cuddled him. Sometimes she heard him crying in his bedroom after she had said goodnight. She would go back in and simply embrace him, allowing him to cry until he fell asleep on her. What else could she do? She felt powerless. His pain cut her inside. After all, Rozi had died to save her life. Karin didn't know how she could come to terms with this, ever. She had not faced it in her writing yet. It was too overwhelming. Maybe one day she would. There was much to deal with, and she felt herself releasing it every day. Karin lay down on her mattress. She pictured Farhan's face and his broad, white smile, which made her feel safe, and she chose to reject other images that sought to come into her mind. She slipped into a deep and peaceful sleep.

***

The next day, she looked at Farhan playing soccer with Yez on the dusty expanse at the end of their street. They ran at the goal together, and Yez kicked the ball between the two shoes they had placed there for the goals.

"Yes! Did you see that, Aunty?" Yez called out to Karin.

"Well done! Good goal." Karin smiled as Farhan turned around and beamed at her.

"Good boy," he said, breathless.

Karin laughed. He wasn't as fit as he thought he was.

They both came over to Karin who was sitting on a step near where they played. Farhan sat down on the small gutter that bounded the street. Yez stood near them, kneeing the ball up in the air and practicing his tricks.

"Can we get an ice cream?" Yez asked.

"Of course," Farhan answered.

They all stood up and walked towards the main street of the town, where they had begun a tradition of buying an ice cream from the store next to the fruit shop.

"Pistachio as usual?" Karin asked, smiling.

"Yes, please," Yez answered.

Yez walked in front of them, kicking and kneeing his ball up in the air. Karin and Farhan walked close to each other. Their hands touched, and they locked their smallest fingers together, but any time someone passed them or came into sight they broke away. Despite the changes to Kobane, it still wasn't acceptable to show affection in public. Karin didn't mind. In private, they were affectionate.

The sun shone on her back and warmed her. She felt better that Yez was showing progress. He still cried sometimes at night for his Mama and Papa, but he was improving during the day. At bedtime, Karin would tell Yez a story she had made up about a brave boy who had adventures and saved people, and she would pray with him. He would fall asleep from weariness on her chest. Seeing Farhan with Yez made her feel so good…he was a good man, and was even becoming like a father to Yez. She was sure that Terah would not have been as good, he was much more selfish and cold. He believed children should be more in the background, and in their own world. Karin glanced over at Farhan and smiled; she was grateful she had been fortunate enough to meet him.

"You look lovely." Farhan said, looking at Karin.

"Thank you," Karin said, looking down at her hands. She had never become accustomed to compliments or how to respond to them. She was getting used to it with him; he often told her how lovely she was with Yez.

"Can you come and visit with my family this weekend?"

"Yes, I think so. Which day?"

"Saturday."

"Yes, that should be fine. Should I be nervous? Do your family like me? I can never tell." Karin laughed a little; she hated feeling self-conscious like this. It seemed harder than battle strategy; negotiating human emotions was excruciating.

"Yes, they love you. Can't you tell?"

"A bit. They seem to like me."

"My mother didn't understand you at first, but now she respects what you have done for Kobane, and for Yez."

Karin felt a pang of guilt flood through her chest. It reminded her of the guilt she felt about Rozi's death.

"Yeah, but there were braver people than me." Farhan took her hand quickly and squeezed it. He knew what she was thinking, as they had talked about this before. Karin felt her throat begin to ache thinking of Rozi now. She became quiet, but she trusted Farhan, and knew she could share her feelings with him.

"I feel horrifying guilt," she said. "At night, I see Roza rising above me, falling onto me, blood everywhere. I feel so angry and guilty that I was spared. She lost her life, and I'm here. It's not right." He touched her arm gently.

"Roza sacrificed herself for me, so did Sozan. I feel the weight of their deaths every day."

"But sweet, you did give up everything for Roza as well," Farhan said. "You gave up your desire to fight." Karin looked ahead at Yez, still playing with his ball. A tear rolled down her cheek, and she wiped it away, not wanting Yez or others to see it.

"Sometimes, I feel like I'm hyperventilating from grief. Sometimes it's so painful to see Yez's expression when I am explaining something to him. I see her face, her manner, and it stabs me. It winds me, like someone has punched me in the stomach. He's just a little boy, and he doesn't have his mother anymore because of me, he doesn't…" Karin's voice faltered.

"It was Daesh that killed Roza. *Not* you. Yez doesn't blame you, sweet." Farhan stopped on the dirt footpath and looked at her.

"Maybe he does, deep down," Karin whispered.

"No. I think he's grateful to you. You can't let this consume you, Kar. Your grief will ease. Your guilt will change in time."

"How do you know, Farhan?" Karin replied, looking straight into his face.

"Because I lost people, too, Kar. I lost my aunt and uncle and I lost my best friend, Daran. You knew him; you met him. He reported with me during the battle, and one day was hit by shrapnel from mortar fire. He was killed right next to me. That haunts me, too. Why didn't I die?"

"I'm sorry." Karin felt her stomach churning. She touched his hand, not caring what people thought. "I am so sorry you lost him. What a good man he was."

"He was the best of men."

They began to walk again to keep up with Yez.

"I'm sorry if I haven't been there for you, enough," Karin said.

"That's okay. You have to be there for Yez."

"Yes, and I know you're right; it will change over time. It will never go away, but it will change. Thanks for being there for me, Far. You know I love you, don't you?" she whispered.

Farhan smiled his white-water smile, and she smiled as well.

"Yes, I do." He grabbed her hand, squeezed it, and then released it. It comforted Karin to know that he understood her guilt. He, too, had tough feelings; about how he had reported on people who were ultimately killed, when he himself had survived the war. He didn't understand why he was spared, and they weren't. Karin felt so grateful that he was in her life. Another person who had not gone through what she had suffered would not understand. They were approaching the main street now, and cars, motorbikes, even donkeys pulling wooden carts passed them. The din of life increased as they walked.

"Kar, I want to ask you how you feel about us and…" Farhan faltered.

"Mama… I mean Aunty, can you carry my ball?" Yez interrupted. Karin had noticed that Yez sometimes went to call her 'mother.'

"Of course."

She carried his ball, and he came and held her hand as they walked to the main street.

"We can talk about this later," Farhan said, smiling.

"Yes, of course."

Finally, they came to the ice cream shop, and felt the cool air of the shop greet them. It was starting to get warmer in Kobane now. Karin led Yez in, and Farhan followed.

*   *   *

Later that night, after Karin and Farhan had had dinner with Maia and Aster, they went outside to talk. Her parents wanted to see her regularly, and she enjoyed being at home as well, though her new home was with Yez. He put his arm around Karin gently. She felt both excited and nervous; she had confronted Daesh men who were seeking to kill her with fewer nerves than she felt being held by a man who loved her.

"Kar."

"Yes."

"Do you love me?"

"You know I do." He smiled, looking straight ahead. Then he turned towards her.

"I love you."

Karin couldn't believe he finally had said it; he hadn't said it directly before. She smiled at him.

"How do you feel about marriage, Kar?"

"If it's with the right person, I'm for it," she replied.

"I know in the war you renounced it, but I wanted to know how you felt about it now."

"Different. I have Yez to think about now." Karin was starting to feel even more nervous.

"Would you consider marrying me, Kar?"

She had always thought receiving another proposal after Terah was impossible. She had never envisaged this happening again. Her eyes began to fill with tears; she suddenly felt terrible. Roza was dead, and yet, she had somehow found love. It didn't seem right. She looked down.

"What's wrong? Did I say the wrong thing?"

"No, I was thinking of Roza."

"Ah, I understand," Farhan said. Karin knew he truly did.

"In answer to your question, I would definitely want to marry you…" She paused for a few seconds. "In time." Karin smiled at him through her tears.

"Oh, I'm so happy," Farhan said. He embraced her and kissed her head many times. Karin pulled away.

"But there is one thing."

"Yes?"

"If you want me, you have to have Yez as well. I'm all he has now."

Farhan paused and looked into her face. He seemed to be examining her features, and she suddenly felt it could all be over.

"We come together," she said. "Wherever I go, he goes. I won't leave him again."

Farhan smiled his expansive smile.

"Of course. I already love Yez as if he was my own."

He took her in his arms and kissed her on the lips, strongly. Karin let herself surrender to this overwhelming feeling of love, and safety in his arms. They broke apart, and both faced out into the cool, quiet night air.

"We need to give Yez time, though. So, let's wait to get engaged. Too much change, too quickly, will not be good for him."

"I know you're right," Farhan said. "I don't want to wait, but I'll wait as long as we have to." He kissed Karin again softly. She surrendered to his tenderness, and put her head on his shoulder. For the first time in months, she could see clearly a future for herself and Yez, stable, expansive, and full of better things than had gone before. She looked to the sky and could see Roza's knowing smile and cheeky wink. Roza would be feeling so self-satisfied now. Karin nearly laughed out loud but stopped herself. She didn't want Farhan to think she was crazy. *You always wanted me to be with him,* Karin thought speaking to Rozi. *You got your wish.* She winked into the blackness.

Farhan didn't see; he was facing straight ahead. Karin could see his smile curling up at the edges, and thought she saw a tear falling down his cheek.

About the Author

Suzanne is a qualified journalist of more than 20 years' experience. In 2017, Suzanne completed a M.A, Creative Writing at Macquarie University.

Suzanne's short stories and poetry have been published in *Compassion: A Creative Anthology, The Quarry Journal, Grapeshot Magazine, Studio Magazine, Time Off and Heretical* magazines. In 2011, her poem, 'Breathe', received a SCLA Award.

For more information about Suzanne's other books and writing, visit and **www.suzannestrong.com.**

Acknowledgements:

First of all, I want to thank my daughter, Leah for editing my early drafts and supporting me with this novel for more than three years. I wish to thank my Supervisor, Rebecca Griggs for her expert advice and input and for Dr Toby Davidson and Dr Lynne Spender for their insightful and kind words about my book. I would like to thank Hassan Somboli from the Brisbane Kurdish Association who provided me with his enthusiastic support and advice on Kurdish language and culture for the book. Importantly, I want to thank the YPJ Media Centre and the Women's Revolution in Rojava who also helped with some research. Hanna Bohman, kindly read my novel for authenticity checks, as she was a soldier with the YPJ in the war in Syria.

For Saffron Drew, from the Sunshine Coast Council who gave me unwavering support for this book. Throughout the whole process Saffron believed in my book and supported me personally. I am very grateful to her. The Sunshine Coast Council also provided funding for my travel to New York and for editing and development of the novel. I am forever grateful to the council and to Saffron.

I need to thank my personal editors, friends and family who provided valuable input into the development of my novel. You know who you are, I couldn't have done this without you. My editor, Jessica Friedmann thank you for your insightful copy editing and incisive comments.

I wish to acknowledge the Kurdish women who fought and died in these ferocious battles against Daesh and for the rights of women. These formidable, funny and spirited Kurdish women constantly inspire me to be courageous and to go forward in strength. I thank God I was able to research and write this novel. It has been challenging, eye-opening, at times difficult, but ultimately awe-inspiring. In this book, I wish to honor the lives of these Kurdish people and the sacrifices they made.

Printed in Great Britain
by Amazon